SCORCHED

A SMALLTOWN, SERIAL KILLER, ROMANTIC SUSPENSE

A KILLER SERIES
BOOK TWO

ELLE JAMES

TWISTED PAGE INC

Copyright © 2025 by Elle James

All rights reserved.

No part of this book may be reproduced in any form or by any electronic or mechanical means, including information storage and retrieval systems, without written permission from the author, except for the use of brief quotations in a book review.

Without in any way limiting the author's [and publisher's] exclusive rights under copyright, any use of this publication to "train" generative artificial intelligence (AI) technologies to generate text is expressly prohibited. The author reserves all rights to license uses of this work for generative AI training and development of machine learning language models.

ISBN EBOOK: 978-1-62695-611-7

ISBN PAPERBACK: 978-1-62695-613-1

ISBN HARDCOVER: 978-1-62695-614-8

Dedicated to my readers who make my dreams come true by keeping me in the business I love dearly...WRITING! I love you all so much. Thank you for buying my books!
Elle James

AUTHOR'S NOTE

A Killer Series
Chilled (#1)
Scorched (#2)
Erased (#3)
Swarmed (#4)

Visit ellejames.com for more titles and release dates
Join her newsletter at
https://ellejames.com/contact/

SCORCHED

A KILLER SERIES BOOK #2

New York Times & *USA Today*
Bestselling Author

ELLE JAMES

CHAPTER 1

"Caesar Valdez, please return to your seat." Elise Johnson struggled to look calm and keep her voice even. She pushed a hand through her damp hair and sighed. Why was the air conditioner on the fritz again? How could she teach in such stifling heat?

Caesar glared at her and slumped into his assigned seat, grumbling, "I don't know why we have to study history, anyway. It's lame. Only losers care about history."

Elise couldn't blame the students for being fractious. The temperature in the room had to be nearing the mid-eighties. Outside, the South Texas summer had stretched well into the triple digits and it was late October, for heaven's sake!

A transplant from North Dakota, Elise suffered in anything above seventy degrees Fahrenheit.

She sighed. If she could just make it another few

minutes, the day would be done, and they could all go home. "Can anyone tell Caesar why we study world history?"

Ashley Finch flicked her straight strawberry-blond hair over her shoulder and looked down her perfect nose at Elise. "Because teachers like to torture teenagers?"

The students laughed.

Elise nodded, already used to the young people posturing in front of their peers. A cheerleader, Ashley liked to be the center of attention and had no trouble speaking up in class; it got her in trouble often. She never knew when to shut up. After several conferences with Ashley's mother, Elise understood where the girl got her mouth and attitude.

"Thank you, Ashley." She stared into the sea of bored faces, each watching the clock on the wall, waiting for the bell to ring and school to end for the day. "Does anyone know another reason why we might want to study history?"

Alex Mendoza glanced from left to right and inched his hand upward.

As one, the entire class moaned.

Alex was the brainiac of the class. He'd already blown the class curve, earning him the disdain of his less fortunate and less studious classmates.

Elise liked him because he was voracious in his desire to learn and his ability to retain what he'd digested. "Yes, Alex?"

"We study history so that we don't repeat the mistakes of our past. If we don't learn from the past, we are destined to do it all over again." His words started out slow and tentative and sped up as if he were afraid the class would pummel him with spit wads for being so verbose. "Who wants another Hitler or Hussein?"

The bell rang before the class could bombard him with a barrage of answers to his questions.

Students grabbed their books and backpacks and scrambled for the door.

Elise straightened her desk and gathered the quiz papers from a previous class. She liked to be home when the boys got off the bus. As a teacher, she had the latitude to be with her young sons when they got out of school. As a single parent, she liked to maintain a certain amount of stability in their lives. They'd been through so much.

Alex Mendoza and Kendall Laughlin were the last to leave, as usual. The two were best friends and partners on the school newspaper. They went everywhere together—joined at the hip, as Elise's mother would have said before she passed away last year.

Kendall stopped in front of Elise's desk. "Ms. Johnson, remember if you need me to babysit, all you have to do is let me know. I'm available practically anytime, and you're just down the street, so I could ride my bike."

Elise chewed her bottom lip. She hadn't been out

with adults since she'd come to Breuer, Texas, the small traditional German town on the outskirts of San Antonio. "Thanks, Kendall, I'll keep you in mind." For when she actually met some adults she could hang out with after teaching school all day. "Alex, don't let Caesar's comments get you down. You two will go far because you aren't afraid or too lazy to learn."

Alex shrugged. "I wasn't worried. While I'm at Stanford earning my doctorate, Caesar will still be bagging groceries."

"Come on, Alex," Kendall said. "My mom's waiting to take us to the library so we can dig up more scoop on Jack the Ripper."

A chill slithered its way down Elise's spine. "Why are you doing a report on Jack the Ripper?"

"We had to pick someone famous in history, and who wants to do the same ol' same ol'?" Kendall grinned.

Alex rolled his eyes. "It was her idea. I wanted Albert Einstein."

Kendall's eyes glowed with enthusiasm. "There's something about an unsolved mystery that appeals to me." She jerked her head toward the door. "Are we going or not? My mom's probably waiting in the parking lot."

Alex smiled and scooted out the door after Kendall.

After the kids had cleared the room, Elise hurried

down the hallway, her footsteps clicking along the tiled floors. She had to stop at the office where she'd drop off parent permission forms for their field trip to Enchanted Rock at the end of next week.

Elise tried to shake the uneasy feeling creeping across her skin. All of Alex and Kendall's talk of Jack the Ripper brought up memories best forgotten.

Students and teachers milled in and out of the office. Elise had to squeeze through to get to the front desk.

"Hi, Elise." Becky McNabb, the school secretary, looked up from her computer terminal at her desk. "How was class?"

"Challenging," she answered, her tone flat, her lips twisting into a wry grin.

"I don't know how you teachers do it." She glanced back at the computer. "I'd have to shoot myself."

"They have their moments." Both good and bad. Elise handed Becky the stack of crumpled papers. "Could you file these?"

"Sure." She stuck a paper clip on them and laid them on the stack in her inbox. "Hey, don't forget to check your cubby before you leave. You got mail today."

Behind the counter, a plain white envelope leaned to the side of her box. She retrieved it and stuffed it in her purse for later.

The small town was just what she and her boys

had needed. Not much traffic and plenty of room to grow. Most of all, it was a long way from North Dakota. A long way from the past, she'd tried her damnedest to erase. She'd changed her name and her sons' last names to ensure no one could trace them or know their identities. The only people who knew where they'd gone were her sister Brenna and Brenna's FBI husband Nick Tarver—the only people she trusted with her children's lives.

For the past four months, she and her sons had lived in the small Texas town with no one aware of what had happened in North Dakota.

A long funeral procession wound its way down Main Street, bringing traffic to a complete standstill. Elise glanced at the clock on the dash. She had a good fifteen minutes before Luke and Brandon got off the bus and she was only five minutes from home once the procession made it past. After shifting her metallic gray SUV into park, she reached into her purse for the envelope, slipped her fingernail beneath the flap and ripped it open. The sharp edge of the flap sliced into her skin, and she jerked her hand back.

Damn. She hated paper cuts. She dabbed at the dot of blood oozing from her finger and opened the envelope. Inside, she found a single white sheet of paper.

Careful not to bleed on the writing, she unfolded

the paper and flattened it. The message was short. It didn't take Elise long to read the three simple lines.

Dear Alice,

For better or worse, until death do us part.

Let death begin.

Cold consumed her, penetrating straight to her bones.

No. This was a mistake. No one knew her here. No one.

She grabbed the envelope. On the outside, Elise Johnson was written in crisp, clean computer print. There was no postage, and no return address.

Her hands shook so hard that the paper and envelope fluttered from her grip and fell to the seat beside her.

Brenna. I have to call Brenna.

She hesitated for a few seconds. Should she? Married now, Brenna was eight months pregnant with her first child. Should Elise call her and upset her?

The words on the note stared up at her, pushing her past reason. She had to talk to her sister. Brenna would know what to do.

Elise fumbled in her purse for her cell phone, pulled up her list of favorites and pressed the name at the top to connect her with her sister living in Minneapolis.

After four rings, Elise's teeth were chattering, and

she almost threw the phone out the window. "Where is she?"

"Al-Elise?" Brenna was still trying to get used to the different name, but her voice sounded so calm over the line.

"Brenna." Elise Johnson's fingers trembled as she held the phone to her ear with one hand and snatched up the letter in the other.

"What's wrong?" Her younger sister had a way of reading her voice, even from over a thousand miles away.

"Brenna. I'm scared."

"Are the boys okay?" Brenna's voice, clear and crisp, snapped over the line.

"The boys are f-fine." Elise sucked in a deep breath and fought back the sob rising in her throat. Fear clenched a hand around her gut and squeezed. "I got a letter today."

"From whom?"

As the procession of cars crawled by one by one with their headlights on like so many zombies, Elise whispered, "I don't know."

"What did it say?"

For several seconds, Elise stared down at the boxy print, her hand shaking so hard, she couldn't read the words. But then, she didn't have to. She could recite them word for word without seeing the paper.

"Elise!" At Brenna's shout, Elise pulled herself together.

She took a deep breath. "The letter said, 'Dear Alice, for better or for worse, until death do us part. Let death begin.'"

"What the hell does that mean?" A street cop turned detective, Brenna didn't tone down her words. "And who the hell knows you're Alice?"

"I don't know. But I'm so scared I can't think." A car honked behind her. Elise jumped and glanced around, realizing the funeral procession had passed and traffic had resumed, except where she held up a dozen cars. "I'm in traffic and I have to go. I'll call you when I get home." She wished her sister was there in Texas, where she could go straight to her.

"Do that. And Elise, don't worry. We'll figure this out."

God, she hoped so. This all had to be a big mistake—a really big mistake. The letter was much like the ones Brenna had received in North Dakota when she'd been on the trail of a serial killer.

That serial killer had turned out to be none other than Elise's husband. He'd very nearly killed Brenna. Hysterical laughter bubbled up in her throat. What woman ever suspected her husband of being a serial killer? Especially a deacon in the church, a man most of the community looked up to and trusted.

They'd told her Stan had died in the fire he'd set in his attempt to kill Brenna. Elise still had nightmares about that time. She'd almost lost her only sister.

Elise had always wondered if Stan really died in that fire.

Memories flowed in like the floodwaters of the Red River that had swept away the burning house with Stan inside two years ago. No body had been recovered, but then he'd been burned and carried away, so what had they expected to find?

Her husband, the serial killer, was dead.

Elise shifted the car into gear and pulled forward, suddenly overwhelmed with the need to hug her children. She wished she had someone big and strong to hug her.

How could anyone know where she was? How could he have found out her secret? Was it really Stan?

Damn it. Stan Klaus *had* to be dead.

Elise couldn't live through all that again.

Then again...maybe that was the plan.

PAUL FLETCHER STEPPED out into the bright afternoon sun. The heat radiating off the pavement warmed his air conditioner-chilled arms. The contrast between the conference room inside and the South Texas heat had to be at least thirty degrees. He might never acclimate if he didn't get out of the office more often.

He marveled at the number of trucks in the parking lot. Hardly anyone in the urban areas of the

East Coast owned pickups. Paul had succumbed to the lure of the four-wheel drive vehicle within a week of arriving and bought a pewter-gray 4x4 truck, glad he'd passed on shiny black like the SUV parked in the space next to his. It looked good, but in the Texas sunshine, black absorbed more heat, making it blistering hot in the long, searing summers.

Before he stepped off the curb onto the sticky black asphalt, Melissa Bradley's bright red truck pulled up next to him. Her automatic window slid down. "Get in."

"Why? I was on my way to the house for a cold beer."

"Change of plans."

Paul climbed into the passenger seat, the dream of relaxing by the apartment complex pool with a beer fading as Melissa pulled onto Interstate 10, headed toward El Paso. "Where are we going?"

"Breuer." Dressed in jeans and dingo boots, Melissa had made the transition from the East Coast like she'd been born and raised in Texas. She'd even picked up a little of the local dialect.

"Why Breuer?"

"Remember Alice Klaus?" She glanced at him before returning her attention to the San Antonio afternoon traffic. Slowing, she allowed drivers from the access ramp to ease onto the busy interstate, headed to the suburbs after a day at work.

"Alice from the Dakota Strangler case in North Dakota?" An image of a pretty lady with pale blond hair and two cute little boys swam into his head. "The wife of the serial killer Alice?"

"That's the one."

"What does she have to do with Breuer?"

"Her sister, Brenna, called a few minutes ago. Apparently, Alice Klaus, now Elise Johnson, settled in Breuer and hired on as a high school history teacher."

A smile lifted the corners of Paul's lips. He remembered her all right. Pretty blonde, killer husband. "She changed her name." He nodded. "A good thing."

"Yeah. Only someone's found her."

Paul tensed and sucked in his breath. "Found her or killed her?" He'd barely known the woman for more than a few days, but he remembered feeling regret. If the circumstances had been different, she was someone he wouldn't mind getting to know better.

Melissa shot a glance at Paul. "Found. She's alive."

Paul let the air out of his lungs and leaned back in his seat for the twenty-minute drive to the hill country outside San Antonio.

When they pulled onto Main Street in Breuer, Paul scanned the small town with a critical eye. White limestone buildings intermingled with old, German-style gingerbread houses. People smiled and waved to each other from the sidewalks and children played in their front yards. Paul would bet most residents didn't even lock their doors at night.

A veritable nightmare if a killer ran loose in their midst.

"Here's Highland Street." Melissa turned left onto the street lined with gnarled live oaks whose branches shaded the curbs, giving the impression of a leafy arched bower instead of a city street.

Melisa parked in front of a yellow cottage with a three-foot-tall, white picket fence surrounding the yard, front and back. "How cute. Reminds me of my grandmother's house in Wisconsin."

Paul dropped down from the passenger side of the truck and pushed through the rickety gate. Before he got halfway to the house, two little boys burst through the front door and raced out into the yard.

"Luke, Brandon! Come back inside right now!" A beautiful woman with long blond hair flung the screen door open and raced out onto the porch, a worried frown creasing her forehead. When she spied Paul, she stopped, her eyes widening. She pressed a hand to her mouth as tears bubbled up and spilled over.

Somewhere in her past life, she had to have been the high school beauty queen. She was so perfect in every way except the tears now pouring down her cheeks.

For a man who avoided crying females like the

plague, Paul couldn't resist moving forward and taking her into his arms. "Shh." He smoothed her hair and spoke to her in a soothing tone. "Everything's going to be okay."

"He's supposed to be dead." She pushed away to stare up into Paul's eyes. Her jaw clenched, angry light refracting off her tears. "He's supposed to be dead."

CHAPTER 2

Elise clutched his shirt like she was grasping for purchase on the face of a drop-off. She felt like she had fallen over the edge of a cliff, straight into her past.

Just seeing Paul and Melissa made the memories of the nightmare all too vivid. These two talented FBI agents had been in Riverton and assisted in the investigation that ultimately identified the Dakota Strangler as Stan Klaus, Elise's husband. During the evacuation of the flooded town of Riverton, Paul had been the one to help get her, the boys and her aging mother out of the evacuation center when the press converged on her.

The solid wall of Paul's chest and the security of his arms triggered all the emotions she'd repressed. All the fear, desperation and disbelief rushed in and threatened to swamp her.

Elise had held it together for the boys, but now that help had arrived, sobs rose in her throat, and she pressed her mouth to his chest to keep from crying out and scaring the children. She needed to stay strong for the boys, but so far, she wasn't doing a good job of it. Her shoulders shook with the force of her sobs as she huddled in Paul's arms, wanting to stay hidden from the world.

"Hey, boys," Melissa said behind her. "Why don't you show me that swing set I see in your backyard? Think I can swing on it?"

From the corner of her eye, she saw Brandon run around Paul's side and stare up at the man, his eyes narrowed into tight slits. "Did you make my mother cry?"

"No, I didn't." Thankfully, Paul shielded Elise from her son's view.

"Did you hurt her?" the boy demanded, his voice rising.

"No sir."

Elise gulped back more tears and tried to collect herself enough to face her oldest son.

Brandon crossed his arms over his little chest. "Let my mother go."

"It's okay, Brandon. Paul's a nice guy," Elise said into Paul's damp shirt, her sobs drying and turning into hiccups.

"Let her go." Brandon stuck his hands between them and attempted to split them apart.

Paul glanced to Melissa for help.

"Let her go!" Brandon's rage turned to tears when all his attempts to separate them resulted in nothing. He balled his fists and beat against the backs of Paul's legs.

Elise pushed away from the warmth of Paul's arms and squatted next to Brandon, gathering him close. Luke edged in on the hug, his little face creased in a frown to match his brother's.

Melissa lifted him into her arms. "Come here, little man."

Elise's lack of control over her emotions made her sons uneasy. Both boys needed reassurance as much as she did, if not more. She was the adult. Adults must be strong. Then why the hell did she feel like she was falling apart?

"It's okay, Brandon. Paul's not hurting me." She scrubbed at the tears on her cheeks and pushed her hair back from her forehead. "I'm okay. I was crying because I was so happy to see Paul and Melissa. Do you remember them?"

In the circle of his mother's arms, Brandon glared from Paul to Melissa, his gaze returning to Paul as if he expected Paul to make another move on his mother.

Elise had never told Brandon why his father had died in a fire or that he was a bad man. She had told him that he was now the man of the house. It was up to him to help her. He'd taken his responsibilities seriously over the past two years, sometimes forgetting it was okay to be an eight-year-old boy.

Kendall Laughlin pulled up beside the picket fence on her bicycle and braked to a halt. "Hi, Ms. Johnson. Hi, Luke. Yo, Brandon."

Luke squirmed in Melissa's arms. "Kenny!" Melissa set the child on his feet, and he was off like a shot and through the gate. "I have a bike now. You wanna see?" He grabbed her hand and pulled her toward the gate.

Kendall laughed and smiled down at the six-year-old boy. "Let me get off mine first." She shot a curious look at Elise. "Is everything okay?"

Elise stood, her hand lingering on Brandon's shoulder. "Yes, Kendall, everything's okay." *My world is catching up to me and my killer husband might be alive, but everything's just fine and dandy*. She attempted a smile that turned into a grimace. "Kendall, could you do me a big favor?"

"Sure." She climbed off her bike and rolled it into the yard.

"Could you watch the boys for a few minutes while I talk to...my old friends, Paul and Melissa?" *And please don't ask too many questions*. Her students couldn't know about her past. Her principal couldn't know, or her peaceful life would be shattered. Who wanted the wife of a serial killer teaching children in their school? Elise had never hurt another human in her life. But her husband had killed five people that she knew of.

"I'd love to. Luke and I are old friends already. Aren't we, buddy?" She ruffled the boy's hair.

Luke jumped up and down. "Come see my new bike."

Brandon stuck by Elise's side, his hand creeping into hers. "I don't want to play."

"Go with Kendall. I promise, everything's okay." She stared down into her son's eyes. "As the man of the house, you need to help me keep an eye on your brother."

His face scrunched into a fierce pout, and he glared again at Paul. "Kendall can watch him."

"She doesn't know all his hiding places." She let go of his hand. "You do. So, it's up to you to keep your brother safe and in the yard. Neither one of you is to leave the yard, understand?"

Brandon nodded.

She patted his shoulder instead of bending down to hug him close. He wouldn't appreciate being treated like a child in front of the other adults. "I need a few minutes to talk to Mr. Fletcher and Ms. Bradley, alone."

"Come on Brandon," Luke called out. "You can show Kenny your new bike, too." With Kendall's hand clutched in his, Elise's youngest son tugged the teen across the yard, grabbed his brother's hand and headed for the back.

Brandon pulled loose of Luke's grip and gave his mother one last look as if to say, *Are you sure?*

Elise nodded, a reassuring smile plastered to her face. "Go on, honey. We'll be in the house."

Dragging his feet, Brandon followed Luke and Kendall around the side of the house to the shed where the bicycles were stored.

Paul's gaze followed the boys. When they were out of sight, he turned to Elise. "Want to show me the note?"

The mention of the note set her heart racing again. If she could, she'd have burned it and scattered the ashes to the winds, as if by doing so, her troubles would blow away. "It's in the house."

She led the way into the living room, taking no pleasure in all the warm and colorful furnishings that were so different than the Spartan look Stan had preferred. The note had turned her happy and sunny home into a sinister place where evil lurked, waiting to pounce. She crossed to the kitchen and glanced out the window.

Brandon and Luke had their bicycles out of the shed. Kendall smiled and laughed with the boys, admiring their new wheels.

Elise pulled the letter out of her purse and held it out for Paul to see. "I don't know what to make of it, but I'll tell you... it has me scared."

Paul pulled a rubber glove from his hip pocket and stretched it over his large, capable hand before he took the note from her. He turned it over, inspecting the outside of the envelope. "Where did you find it?"

"It was in my mailbox cubby at school today." Elise spun away and paced across the ceramic kitchen tiles. This was her home, a place where she could make new friends and her boys could grow up unencumbered by their father's crimes.

Fear turned to anger.

She marched back across the tile to face the two agents. "Tell me, guys. What really happened to Stan? Did he, or did he not die in that fire?"

* * *

PAUL REMEMBERED the shock and disbelief in Elise's face after she'd learned what her husband had done two years ago.

She'd suffered through the stares and whispers of the people she'd sat beside in church for years. They'd shunned her as if she'd been the one to kill those innocent women. They couldn't understand how her husband could have committed all those crimes with her unaware. Didn't she live in the same house?

Paul had heard the whispers, the catty remarks and the name-calling. When the reporters descended on her, he'd been there to get her out and relocate her to a private room where she, the boys and her mother remained out of the spotlight. All the while, she'd put up a strong front for Brandon and Luke, shielding them from the ugliness as best she could. They had been too young to understand and hopefully too young to remember.

Now, Elise's blue eyes blazed, the anger a welcome change from the defeated and frightened young woman of a moment ago.

He stared down at the letter, like so many others he'd seen on the case in Riverton, North Dakota. Had Stan Klaus lived through the fire and flood? They'd never found his body. "We'll have the letter examined by our lab."

Melissa pulled out an evidence bag from her back pocket and opened it.

Paul dropped the letter inside. "What did it say?"

Elise inhaled through her mouth, her lip quivering ever so slightly. "Dear Alice, for better or for worse, until death do us part. Let death begin." She said it in a flat, emotionless tone. When she finished, her body trembled from head to toe.

"Alice? He specifically said, 'Dear Alice'?" Melissa asked.

Elise nodded. She'd put that name behind her, even went so far as to consider her old self as someone who'd died along with Stan. Alice Klaus had been young, naïve and stupid. Elise Johnson was savvy, aware and would never harbor a killer in her home. Ever.

"Have you or the boys told anyone your former names?"

"No. The two years we spent in Minneapolis gave us time to adjust to the new names. When we moved here, we started our new lives. No one knows who we are."

Melissa snorted. "Someone does."

"Question is who?" Paul held the evidence bag up. "Who would write a note like that and for what purpose?"

"Could be just a scare tactic." Melissa shrugged. "Who have you made mad since you moved here?"

Elise shook her head, her brow furrowing. "One of my student's parents, or maybe a student?"

Paul cocked an eyebrow. "A student?"

"I have a bully and a talker," Elise said. "I sent the talker to detention for two days straight. Her mother read me the riot act, claiming I was denying her daughter an education, although she gets the same work at the detention center as in the classroom. In fact, she gets more. The only thing she doesn't get is cheer practice and she's benched for the next game."

"Do you think that student could be using your past against you?" Paul asked.

"Ashley?" Elise shook her head. "She's more interested in her next boyfriend than exacting revenge on a teacher."

Melissa's mouth thinned. "You'd be surprised what kids can do."

Elise pressed her fingers to her temples. "I'd be more afraid of her mother than Ashley. Gerri Finch is a nightmare in heels. Your basic overachieving stage mother."

Melissa stared across the evidence to Paul. "Wouldn't hurt to question her."

Elise looked from Melissa to Paul. "Does that mean you're taking the case? Or should I have turned this into the police?"

"Technically, we don't have a case," Melissa said. "No one's been hurt."

"Yet. That's the whole idea. I don't want anyone else hurt by my husband or whoever sent this. I don't want to be responsible for any more murders."

Paul lifted one of Elise's hands. "Elise, your husband murdered those women, not you."

She pulled her hand from Paul's grasp. "I should have seen through those late-night service calls." She threw her arms in the air. "At the very least, I should have suspected *something*. Good God, I lived with the man. The manipulative, verbally abusive, domineering son of a—"

"You weren't the only one who trusted him. He had an entire community snowed." Melissa moved up beside Paul. "In most cases involving serial killers, the people closest to them never saw it coming."

Elise rolled her eyes, a shaky laugh erupting from her throat. "Oh, that makes me feel so much better about the women my husband killed."

"I know it's not much. But it took us a while to figure him out as well." Melissa gave her a crooked smile. "Hell, we were almost too late to save your sis—"

"Mel, let me handle this," Paul said.

Melissa's face turned pink, and she backed away. "Yeah, maybe you should."

Elise's frown returned. "Look, I don't want either of you to feel like you're walking on eggshells around me. I don't need people feeling sorry for me any more than I want their blame for the deaths. After two years, I've managed to start over and put the horror behind me. Or so I thought. Will I ever be free of Stan Klaus?"

Melissa touched her arm. "Yes. At least you should be free of him. Like you said, he's supposed to be dead."

"Elise," Paul said, "for now, we're going to do some checking without opening a case. The local police would be handling this one if we were to turn it in, which we might do soon if we need their help."

"I'd rather the locals didn't know any more than they have to," Elise said. "We have to live here. I can't keep uprooting my children and moving every time someone recognizes me."

"Or threatens you and your children," Paul added.

Her face blanched. She drew in a deep breath and let it out. "If my husband is still alive, he'll come after his sons. I won't let him have them. I swear I'll kill the monster first."

* * *

PAUL AND MELISSA rode back to San Antonio in silence, with Paul immersed in his memories of North Dakota and the first contact he'd had with Alice Klaus. He remembered thinking how unfair life was to dump this horrific burden on such a nice woman and her kids. He'd gone to the evacuation shelter and played with Brandon and Luke to help her out and give her a break while her hometown flooded, and her life fell apart.

She'd been strong then, but now he recognized her behavior as one of a person in shock and denial. The Texas sunshine had done her good, tanning her pale northern skin. She was too young to be widowed and too pretty to live alone. Elise Johnson needed a man around to run interference for her and provide some kind of protection. Either that or a gun.

The sound of little boys shouting in the backyard had grounded Paul in Elise's reality. A gun in the house wasn't a good idea either. Not with curious boys on the loose.

Stan had set fire to the house he supposedly died in. When Paul, Melissa, Nick and Brenna left the house, the river had already flooded the road, and the house had been a raging inferno. By the time they'd been able to return, the house had been swept away in the floodwaters. Stan's vehicle had been found along the banks of the Red River, five miles south of Riverton. Empty.

Had Stan Klaus survived? If so, why had he showed up now? Why not sooner?

Paul turned to Melissa. "Until we get something solid to go on, I want this case kept between you and me."

"You're the boss." Melissa gave him a mock salute. "It really is hard calling you boss."

"You didn't have to take this assignment, you know. And if you recall, I tried to talk you out of it."

"And miss my one and only opportunity to transfer to Texas?" She gunned the accelerator of her cherry-red F150 four-wheel drive pickup. "I'd take a job with the devil himself just to leave the snow behind."

At 7:00 p.m., Paul entered the Bureau building in San Antonio and headed for his office, Melissa close on his heels.

As they passed Special Agent Trevor Cain's desk, the agent looked up from his conversation on the telephone. His eyes widened and he smiled up at them. "*Muy bien. Adios,*" he said into the receiver and hung up. "Hey, Bradley, Fletch. Where've you been?" Cain rose from his desk and followed them down the hall.

"Cain." Paul acknowledged the man with a nod before he entered his office.

"You're pulling a late night," Melissa commented, standing in the door. "Still working on those applicant background investigations?"

"Yeah." Trevor Cain moved as if to enter, but Mel wasn't in a hurry to make way. She crossed her arms and leaned against the doorjamb, effectively blocking his entrance.

Thank goodness Mel had decided to transfer to San Antonio with Paul. She understood him, could read him like only a close friend could. Paul smothered a grin.

"Your ability to speak Spanish is a plus around here," Mel commented.

Paul fought impatience. He was ready for the conversation to end and for Cain to disappear so that he could discuss Elise with Mel.

Cain shrugged, his attention focused on Paul. "It comes in handy."

"Making any headway?" Paul asked.

"Some. There are just so many, it doesn't feel like it. I'd rather sink my teeth into something more interesting."

"We all do our jobs." Paul refused to be drawn into another discussion about what FBI agents should be doing. He knew Trevor wanted a case more substantial than applicant background checks, but everyone had to do them. Trevor just needed to do his share.

Cain snorted. "We can't all get the national headliners like you two, huh?" His tone held more of a bite than just another agent joking with his comrades.

"No, we can't." Paul glanced at Melissa. "Could you close my door? I have some calls to make."

"Will do." Melissa closed the door, luring Trevor away.

Paul owed her for that one. Trevor might be a good agent, but he was too impatient for the next big case. What he seemed to forget was that when they got a big case, it meant people were being either kidnapped or murdered. While Trevor was looking for a thrill, others were just trying to survive or keep someone else from being hurt.

Trevor had a lot to learn about being a good agent. In his new supervisory role, Paul hoped he'd have the patience to teach the man.

For now, he wanted to fish and see if Elise's note had more guts behind it than just paper and ink.

His first call was to the Kendall County Sheriff's Department. Now, how did he phrase his question in a manner that wouldn't raise too much suspicion?

"Kendall County Sheriff's Department."

Paul identified himself, stating his position with the FBI in the San Antonio field office.

"What can I help you with, Agent Fletcher?" the woman asked.

"Have there been any missing persons reported in the past forty-eight hours, particularly women?"

After a long pause, the woman spoke. "No, sir. Do you want me to notify you if something should come up in that respect?"

"Yes, please." He gave her his number, hung up and repeated his query at the sheriff's office for the next county over and got the same response. So far, so good. Maybe there wasn't anything to the note after all.

His gut told him differently, and his gut was rarely wrong.

A light knock sounded at the door and Melissa stuck her head in. "Mind if I join you?"

"Trevor head home?" he countered.

"No, he's at his desk, slogging through more background checks." She chuckled. "He's not at all happy about it either."

"He'll get over it." Paul tipped his head to the side. "Come in."

Melissa entered, sinking into the seat across from Paul's desk. "What are you going to do about the note?"

"I made a few calls to outlying counties. I haven't called the Bexar County Sheriff or San Antonio Police Department yet. They're next on my list."

"What exactly are you asking them?"

"I'm inquiring about missing persons reported in

the past forty-eight hours." He glanced at Melissa. "You got any other ideas?"

"I'll run the envelope and letter over to Forensics to see if we can lift any prints."

"Thanks."

"What do you think? Is it a real threat or a prank?"

Paul tapped a pencil to his desk blotter. "I don't know. But I have a bad feeling about it. Elise and her kids are on their own. Vulnerable."

"Why don't you assign an agent to them?"

"A note isn't enough to go on. By rights, it should be a local case, not even in FBI jurisdiction."

"Unless Stan Klaus really is alive and up to his old tricks again."

The phone on Paul's desk rang. "Let's hope not."

Paul lifted the receiver. "This is Fletcher."

"Agent Fletcher, this is Rita at the Kendall County Sheriff's office. We just had a woman reported missing. Last seen at ten o'clock last night. Normally, a missing persons report isn't filed until twenty-four hours after the person has supposedly gone missing, but you wanted to know."

CHAPTER 3

ELISE SPENT two hours lying in bed that night, willing herself to sleep, but with very little luck. Shortly after midnight, due to sheer exhaustion, she dozed off.

The dream started when she was a teenager, back during the first flood when her family evacuated Riverton. Her father, mother and sister were all there, alive and well. The dream transitioned into the flood of two years ago, when the Riverton Police Department and the FBI were hot on the case of a serial killer.

They didn't know who it was, but she did. She was lying in bed next to her husband in her house in North Dakota. Her husband was the killer, but he didn't know she knew. Terrified, she lay there, afraid to look at him lest he see in her eyes that she knew. When she worked up the courage and looked at Stan, he was gone.

Afraid for her boys, she leaped out of bed and ran down the longest hallway of her life. She didn't remember the hall being that long, but the more she ran, the longer it became. When she finally reached the boys' room and peered inside, their beds were empty, and floodwaters had seeped through the walls.

She searched through the house, the water rising from her ankles to her knees, dragging at her nightgown, pulling her down. With water up to her waist, she couldn't find the front door to the house. Where were the boys? They weren't good swimmers. Had Stan taken them? Would he murder his own sons like he'd murdered those women?

When she finally found the front door, she grabbed the handle beneath the surface of the water and pulled, but the door wouldn't open. The water kept it from moving and had risen to just below her chin.

"Help!" she cried. "Help me!" No one heard her, no one came. When the water covered her face, the door opened and she poured out into the cold, dark street. The flood had only been in her house. The streets were dry and everyone was gone.

She was completely alone.

Elise knew in her heart it was all a dream, but when the fear and emptiness threatened to choke off her air, she forced herself awake. She was the only one who could stop the nightmare from sucking her into a black abyss of despair. She was the only one who could make the evil go away.

At two o'clock, she woke, her body shaking. The covers had slid to the floor and the air conditioner had done an excellent job of keeping the house cool. Too cool.

A subtle creaking sound reached her from the living room. Was someone in the house or was she going to start imagining that every noise was Stan trying to break into her home?

She slid her feet over the edge of the bed and stepped onto the floor, glad it was dry and not flooding like the house in her dream.

Padding quietly down the hallway, she confirmed both boys were still in the house. As if they sensed their mother's restlessness, they'd tossed off the covers from their matching twin beds. She tucked them in, kissed their foreheads and trudged back to her room.

By four o'clock, Elise gave up her pretense of sleeping, afraid she'd go right back to the same nightmare. Instead, she paced for the next couple of hours, working through every possible scenario.

If the note wasn't from Stan, who would be sick enough to send it to her? Since it hadn't gone through the postal system, someone who had access to the school had to have left it there. How many people could she have angered in the past few months? Angry enough to send her threatening notes? One of her students? A parent? The garbage man? Her next-door neighbor? Who? Her head ached, and she still hadn't come up with one viable suspect.

Instead of letting the boys ride the bus that morning, she dropped them off at school. If Stan were alive, he'd want his boys. How could she keep them safe? She couldn't stay home and lock the doors forever, could she?

Before the boys got out of the car, she warned them that she was the only person allowed to pick them up and they were not to talk to strangers. Ever.

Brandon nodded, his face somber.

Luke bounced out of the car, shouting, "Okay, Mom."

On her drive to work, she almost wrecked when she saw a man who vaguely resembled Stan. She circled the street, looking for him, but he'd disappeared. By the time she arrived at the school, she swore she'd seen at least a dozen Stan Klaus look-alikes.

This is crazy! How could she live like this, scared of every man with brown hair and brown eyes.

Afraid someone would stop her in the hallway and ask her what was wrong, she ducked into her classroom and hid behind her computer, hoping no one would talk to her before class started. What could she say? *I'm not sleeping well because my demented, serial-killer husband is not dead like I thought.*

Ten minutes before the bell rang for second period and Elise's first class, Gerri Finch flounced into the room, a sullen Ashley in tow. "Ms. Johnson, what do you mean by giving my Ashley three tardies in your class?"

At barely eight in the morning, after a sleepless night of worry, Elise was in no mood to put up with Gerri. "Did you ask Ashley?"

"Don't get flippant with me. I pay your salary out of the god-awful amount of taxes I pay each year. Don't think I can't pull the plug on your little vendetta against my little girl."

Elise would bet Gerri Finch hadn't worked a day in her life and if she had, she hadn't paid a dime of taxes. As the general manager of one of the larger auto dealerships in San Antonio, her husband raked in a six-figure salary plus bonuses, enabling him to keep his wife and daughter in the manner to which they'd become accustomed.

"Oh, Mom." Ashley tugged against her mother's clawlike grip. "Just leave it."

"I will not. She's been out to get you since the first day of school and I won't have it." Gerri's voice rose with each word she said until she was yelling.

"Ms. Finch, my class starts in five minutes. Unless you plan to stay and keep quiet, I suggest you take your complaint to the principal's office." To Ashley, she said, "You've been late to class five times. The rule says three tardies and you're in Saturday school. I gave you two freebies." Elise raised her brows at the girl. "Didn't I, Ashley?"

Ashley shrugged instead of answering.

Gerri stepped between Ashley and Elise. "If she goes to Saturday school, she'll miss the cheer competition. She's captain of the cheerleading squad, for heaven's sake."

"Then maybe she should set the example for her peers and get to class on time." Elise stood and herded the mother and daughter toward the door where students waited to get in. "I'm following the rules, Mrs. Finch. Now, if you'll excuse me, the bell is about—"

As Elise opened the classroom door, the ear-splitting school bell blared in the hallway.

Teenagers filed in, looking no more rested than she felt but probably possessing a lot more energy.

Elise braced herself for the day ahead, wondering if she'd get a moment to call Paul and Melissa for an update.

Gerri glared at her over the heads of the teens. "I'll take this matter to the principal. Just you wait. We're not through yet."

Oh, goody. One more thing to worry about. As if she didn't have enough on her mind with a death threat. She stared after Gerri Finch. Could the pushy mother be the one who'd sent her the letter? She certainly had access to the school. She volunteered on occasion and knew every teacher by name.

Elise made a mental note to talk to Paul about Gerri. In the meantime, she had a full day of teaching to get through before she could meet up with the FBI agents later that afternoon.

The day passed much like the others in her teaching job. With the added stress of the note, she fought to be patient with the teens. Every minor thing was a major problem to them. Drama, always drama. The "me" mentality wouldn't let them see past their own little worlds to the bigger, harsher world outside Breuer, Texas.

On good days, Elise put herself in their shoes and tried to empathize, but today...not a chance. What to wear to the football game on Friday was the last thing she considered important.

How to survive a serial killer ranked just a bit higher on her list.

If the constant chatter wasn't bad enough, Caesar Valdez was up to his usual tricks, as well, in her last class of the day. Her challenging class, as the seasoned teachers called it. The young man couldn't sit still to save his life. After Elise had told him to return to his seat for the fourth time, she snapped.

"Caesar, I can't teach when you constantly interrupt the class. Go to the principal's office. You can spend the rest of the week in the Student Alternative Center."

Caesar stood, puffed out his chest and said, "No."

Elise blinked, surprised by his blatant refusal to do as he was told. "What do you mean by no?"

He shrugged, his lip curling into a sneer. "No."

The bell chose that moment to ring, indicating the end of the longest day of Elise's life.

While most of the students grabbed their books and raced for the door, Caesar stood his ground.

"That's fine, Caesar. I'll inform the principal of your behavior. She can deal with it."

"Why don't *you* deal with it?" He stepped forward until he was only two feet away from her.

Her personal space threatened, Elise refused to back down. "Just because you're bigger than me, doesn't mean you can push me around, Caesar. Back off."

"You heard her, Caesar. Back off." Kendall dropped her backpack on her desk and stepped up beside Elise.

"That's right. We're tired of you pushing people around." Alex moved to stand on Elise's other side.

Caesar's brows rose at the united front. After a quick glance around at the room still full of his peers, Caesar's glare returned. "You three don't scare me. You can't do anything to me."

"Maybe they can't, but I can." Paul Fletcher stepped through the doorway and stood a good six inches taller than Caesar. His muscular chest was developed and solid. Not to mention, Paul was a trained federal agent, and he looked like it, from the way he stood to the cold look he directed toward Caesar.

Elise let the breath out that she'd been holding. Glad for the interference, she knew she'd ultimately pay for not dealing with the problem herself. Now that Paul had stepped in, Caesar would find another time to test her and possibly Kendall and Alex. Not good.

Caesar stared at Paul as if weighing his options and then he shrugged. "I got better things to do." He pushed past Paul and left the room.

"You okay?" Paul looked at her with a concerned frown.

With a half dozen students still gawking, she squared her shoulders and nodded. "Yes. I'm fine. Just another day in the classroom." She shot a glance at the teens still standing around, her eyebrows rising. "Don't you have homes to go to?"

They ducked their heads and scurried out the door, except for Alex and Kendall.

"I can't believe what Caesar tried to pull. Someone needs to take him down." Kendall threw back her shoulders as if she'd like to be the one to do it—all five-foot-two girl with attitude. "We've got enough going on around here without him playing the class jerk."

Elise grabbed Kendall's arm. "You be careful around him. He's got a lot more bulk to him than you, and apparently, he's not afraid to throw it around."

"He doesn't scare us," Alex said, standing as tall as his five-foot-four-inch frame would go. "I'm a black belt in Tae kwon do."

"Yeah, but he has eighty pounds on you," Elise reminded him.

The teen's eyes narrowed. "Doesn't matter how big you are. What matters is how you use what you have."

"Yeah," Kendall added. "I took self-defense, too." When Alex shot her a surprised look, she blushed. "My dad insisted." Kendall's brows rose. "It could happen to anybody, look at that woman who disappeared last night. She was taken from her home right here in Breuer."

The blood in Elise's head rushed to her stomach and she swayed. "A woman disappeared?" She frowned at Kendall. "How did you know?"

"My dad works for the sheriff's department." Kendall laughed. "I guess the cop thing runs in the family."

Elise's gaze connected with Paul's. "Did you know about this?"

Paul nodded. "I got word about it last night."

Heat rose in Elise's cheeks. Instead of blasting Paul, she turned calmly toward the teens. "Kendall, Alex, did you need me for anything?"

"No, ma'am," Kendall responded.

Kendall and Alex left Paul and Elise alone in the classroom with the door half-closed.

Paul visibly braced himself.

As well he should.

As soon as the kids were out of earshot, Elise launched her attack. "Why didn't you call me?"

"We don't know whether or not the woman's disappearance had anything to do with the note," Paul said.

"Still, I want to know what's going on." She paced across the classroom and back, only to stop directly in front of him. "I can't believe you didn't tell me. How could you? You know what it means to me."

"Exactly." Paul's lips twisted. "If I'd told you about the woman, you wouldn't have slept a wink."

"You think I slept last night?" She dropped her voice to just above a whisper. "I had nightmares about him all night. This morning, I swear I saw Stan in every face on the street. Is he or is he not dead?"

Paul sighed. "We don't know with absolute certainty."

"That's not good enough, damn it." Her eyes filled with moisture, and she stepped closer. "You don't know what it's like to look over your shoulder every second of the day. Or the hell you go through when you let your children out of your sight to go to school. To school, for heaven's sake." Her voice cracked and tears spilled over the edge of her eyelids and down her face. "Why didn't you make sure he was dead then? If he is alive, what have I done to this town? What have I brought with me by moving here?"

"You haven't brought anything. We don't know if it's your husband or someone playing a prank on you. You have to give us time." He clasped her arms and stared down into her face.

"Time?" She looked up at him through a haze of tears. "Does that missing woman have time?"

A noise at the door drew Paul's attention, saving him from answering.

Kendall stood there, her eyes wide, her hand hovering, as if to knock. "I-I'm sorry. I didn't mean to interrupt." Her glance darted to Elise and then to the desk where her backpack lay. "I forgot something."

"Get it," Elise said through her teeth, turning her back to the girl.

Kendall dove for the backpack and almost made it out the door when Elise swung back.

"Kendall, wait." She scrubbed her hand over her cheeks and frowned at the teen. "How much of our conversation did you overhear?"

The girl eased around. "Not much." She didn't look Elise in the eye when she responded. "I have to go." She spun toward the door.

"Kendall." Paul stepped in front of her. "How much did you hear?"

"Nothing I'll repeat. I swear." Kendall looked around Paul to Elise. "Alex and I like you, Ms. Johnson. You're our favorite teacher. We'd never do or say anything that would hurt you."

Elise stared at her for a long moment. "It's very important that whatever you think you might have heard doesn't go outside this room."

The girl nodded, her eyes wide, scared. "I promise, it won't."

"Go home, Kendall." Elise gave her a crooked smile, but the smile faded, and she added, "And lock your doors."

When the young lady had gone, Elise glanced up at Paul, a worried frown pinching her forehead. "If word gets out about my problem, I'll be kicked out of this school so fast, I won't know what hit my backside."

"I don't think the kid will rat on you." Paul stared into her eyes. "Are you ready to leave?"

"Yes." She glanced around the room one last time as if checking for stray students. "My sons will be home soon."

But she didn't move, yet. "Maybe I should turn in my resignation now and save the school the worry."

"Don't borrow trouble, Elise. You're a good teacher. You have a right to a life."

"Yeah, so do the rest of the people of Breuer." She looked up into his eyes, her jaw tightening. "So did the woman who disappeared."

Paul raised his hands as if to reach for her and then let them drop.

Elise slung her handbag over her shoulder.

Paul gripped her elbow and hurried her out of the classroom and out to the parking lot.

"We'll take my truck." He released his hold on her arm and waved toward a big, dark gray pickup parked in the visitor's parking area.

"No, I'll need my car." When she tried to step around him and go to her car, he snagged her arm.

"That's what I came here to talk to you about." He held the passenger door open. "Before the boys get home, I have something to tell you, and I don't want you driving while I tell you."

"You mean there's more?" She closed her eyes and swayed.

"Yeah. Get in." He all but lifted her into the seat and closed the door. When he'd climbed in beside her and had the door safely shut, he turned in his seat. "They found Lauren Pendley this afternoon. She was the missing woman."

"Oh, God." Elise pressed her fist to her lips, tears welling in her eyes. "Where?"

Paul hesitated.

Elise laid her fist in her lap and raised her chin. "Just tell me."

"They found her in the Guadalupe River bound with Ethernet cable."

His words hit her like a punch in the gut.

"Oh, God, oh, God." Elise wrapped her arms around herself and rocked back and forth in her seat.

"The woman had been strangled, tied with Ethernet cable and dumped, just like the women in the Dakota Strangler case," Paul continued. "One other disturbing item to note," he paused, "she went by Lauren, but her first name was Alice."

CHAPTER 4

ELISE'S EYES BURNED, tears held in check by the cold wash of fear snaking through her body, stiffening her limbs. "It's him."

"We don't know that, but Mel and I will be working with the local sheriff's department and city police to find the man responsible."

"It's him." Her voice sounded hollow, even to her own ears. "He didn't die in the fire."

"That wasn't his usual M.O." Paul shifted into Drive and pulled out of the school parking lot, careful not to hit loitering teens waiting for parents to get off work. "Stan didn't care about first names. He chose smart women."

True. Her grip on the armrest loosened slightly. She no longer believed in coincidence, not since the Dakota Strangler. She wouldn't let herself. "But it's too much of a coincidence. It has to be him." And if it was him, even the kids at school could be in danger, especially the girls.

Elise fumbled for the button to lower the window so that she could shout out a warning to the female students still loitering on school grounds. Her hands shook and the tears filling her eyes made it impossible to see. "How do I open the window?"

Paul brought the truck to a halt. He reached across her lap and laid a hand over her shaking one. "Alice, it'll be all right."

She jerked her face toward his, heat rising up her neck and into her cheeks. "Don't call me that! Alice Klaus is dead as far as I'm concerned. She was stupid and deserved to die along with all the other women her husband killed."

Paul grabbed her hand and kept her from lowering her window. "No. Alice didn't die. You're alive and kicking and living in Texas."

"No, she's not." Her faith in herself had died a little more with each one of the women Stan had murdered. How could this man think she was the same woman?

"Alice—Elise..." He touched a finger to her jaw and turned her to face him. "You're beautiful and smart enough to realize you aren't to blame for what happened. Stan, and only Stan, was responsible."

"How can you say that? I lived with the man. I should have stopped him. Now that maniac is out there. These kids could be in danger. I have to let them know."

"You can't Elise. You'll have an entire town up in arms and like you said, you'll lose your job."

Anger burned in her chest. She wanted to take it out on Paul but knew it wasn't his fault. He'd been nothing but kind to her and her children when her world had shattered. Even back then, she remembered thinking how nice it would have been to be married to a man like Paul—a man who cared enough to protect them from harm.

The steam fizzled out of her. Elise slumped in her seat, pulling her hand free of his. Paul was a nice man. Stan was nice when Elise had married him. But people changed. She'd changed.

She stared out at the lingering teens. She wanted to warn them. Warn everyone that she was the plague. That a killer had followed her all the way to Texas. "It's not right for me to keep this secret. So many could be at risk."

"We can't be certain that Stan did it. We don't know if you or anyone around you is the real target. This could all be a fluke."

"I don't think so." She shook her head and stared out at the stunted live oak trees, gnarled and twisted by weather. "But you're right. I can't leave. I used all my savings to move us to Texas. I don't have any money left to keep running."

"You can't keep running." Paul spoke in low,

steady tones, his voice caressing her with a calm she couldn't manage on her own.

She breathed in and out, willing her heart rate to slow. But then it cranked up again. "We don't know where he'll strike next."

"If he strikes," Paul said.

Elise stared out at the clear blue sky, mocking her dark thoughts. How could it be so bright and sunny when a killer stalked the streets? "We can't let him hurt anyone else." She sat up straighter, squaring her shoulders. Now wasn't the time to go soft. She had to be strong. A glance at the clock made her blood race. "I won't let him take my boys. Can you go a little faster, Agent Fletcher? Their bus will be there in less than five minutes."

"Yes, ma'am." A hint of a smile flashed on Paul's face before he pulled out onto the street, focused on beating traffic.

For the first couple of minutes, she remained silent, her thoughts churning over her options. She didn't have the money to gather her belongings and move to another city. Her house wasn't wired with a security system, and she'd used the last of her meager savings to replace the air conditioner, a must in the blazing heat of a South Texas Indian summer. "Do you think the bank would loan me enough money to install a security system?"

Paul shrugged. "You don't know until you ask."

With a sigh, she forced herself to lean back in her seat. "How long does it take to install one?"

"Depends on the contractor."

Elise snorted softly. "Maybe a gun would be the better investment. More immediate."

"There's usually a waiting period to purchase a gun." He shot a glance at her. "Do you even know how to use one?"

"No." Her lips twisted. "Actually, they scare me."

"And you don't want to risk your boys getting their hands on a loaded gun, and loaded is the only way a gun is of use to you."

Hopelessness washed over her, and she shook her head. "So, what you're telling me is that I'm basically defenseless in my own home."

"Not quite. I have a proposition for you."

Her gaze narrowed on Paul. "What do you mean, a proposition?"

He didn't look at her but kept his attention on navigating the turn into her driveway. "I could stay with you at night until we catch him."

Elise's heart fluttered and her hands grew cold and clammy. She hadn't lived in the same house with a man since she'd left North Dakota. Heck, she hadn't trusted herself with another man since.

The last time she'd been with Paul, he'd played with her children in the evacuation shelter. She'd been drawn to the sexy federal agent more than she wanted to admit but chalked it up to vulnerability.

Tall, blond and incredibly handsome, Paul remained hard to ignore. But that didn't matter. She couldn't get involved with anyone, not now or ever. Not with her track record with men. "No. That's not possible."

Her voice quivered and her hands shook as she fumbled for her seat belt. The interior of the truck suddenly too closed in, the air thick with tension. The scent of Paul's aftershave drifted beneath her defenses, making her think thoughts she hadn't dared to in a very long time.

Before she could climb down, he was out and holding the door for her. He helped her down and held her arms in his hands. "Please reconsider, Elise."

The big, yellow bus turned onto Highland Street, its brakes screeching as it came to a halt halfway down the block. The doors opened and a backpack flew off the bus, landing on the pavement. Luke leaped to the ground, laughing.

Brandon clambered down after him, his gaze shooting immediately to where Elise stood in Paul's arm. His eyes narrowed and he grabbed Luke's hand, hurrying him home.

"You should go." Elise could see the storm brewing in Brandon's eyes.

"Okay, but I'll be back later." He stared down into her eyes. "To stay."

"I'll think about it."

. . .

Paul climbed into his truck, feeling like he was running away when every instinct told him to stay. He, too, had seen the look on Brandon's young face. The little guy had been through enough, losing more than a father. Elise wanted to handle her children her own way. He'd give her the space.

For now.

At least until he could get back to the office and have a powwow with Mel. He hadn't planned on staying with Elise, but he didn't see any other way to protect her during the dark hours when most people slept.

He pulled his cell phone out of his pocket and called the Kendall County Sheriff's Department. "This is Special Agent Fletcher, I'd like to speak to Sheriff Engel?"

He pulled into a church parking lot and waited while the operator made the transfer.

"This is the sheriff. What can I do for you, Agent Fletcher?"

"I'd like to meet with you concerning the woman found murdered."

"This case isn't in your jurisdiction, unless you've got something to share from the FBI?"

"I understand." He'd known he'd have to dance around Elise's connection, but he had to open the lines of communication exchange with the men actually working the case. "We can discuss it in further detail when we meet."

"How's nine o'clock in the morning? The Denny's in Breuer. I'm partial to their chicken-fried steak. Just don't tell my wife I eat it for breakfast. She's trying to get me on some danged low-fat diet."

"Your secret's safe with me." Paul's stomach rumbled at the mention of food. He hadn't eaten since he'd grabbed a biscuit at the McDonald's on his way to work that morning. "I'll be there at nine. Thanks." He clicked the end button and called Agent Melissa Bradley.

"Hey, Fletcher," Melissa answered on the first ring. "How did Alice take the news?"

"Elise. She insists we call her Elise. I just left her house." His grip tightened on the phone. "She's pretty shaken. Wants to buy a gun."

"I would be, too." Mel snorted. "Does she even know how to use one?"

"Not a clue."

"Almost as scary a thought as a serial killer returned from the dead."

"I'm not buying that it's Stan. That house was in flames. If the fire didn't get him, the smoke would have."

"Yeah, but we didn't find the body." Mel's voice dropped to barely above a whisper. "We can't rule it out."

"If he's alive, he had to have been in a hospital for burns or smoke inhalation."

"I'll check with all the hospitals in the Riverton area around that time frame."

"Good. And also check the hospitals farther along the Red River. If Klaus did live, he could have ended up miles downriver."

"Hey, boss, here's a chance for you to get to know Cain's abilities. Want me to get him to help make the calls?"

Paul hesitated. On the one hand, Cain had been itching for a case with more meat. Then again, he still didn't know how much he could trust Cain to keep his mouth shut. Paul had only been on the job for two months, not long enough to get a good feel for the other man's capabilities or loyalties. Not to mention, Cain hadn't been overly pleased with an outsider moving into his territory. "I don't know what to think about Cain, yet."

"What? He hasn't warmed up to the ol' Fletcher charm yet?"

"No, the district coordinator warned me that some of the men had been up for the job I got. I wonder if he was one of them."

"Sour grapes?"

"Could be. I don't want him involved until I get a better feel for his work. Especially with Ali-Ms. Johnson's need for confidentiality."

"Gotcha. Mum's the word around Cain." Mel paused. "You want me to take lead on this one, boss?"

"No, I'll take lead."

"Not trying to overstep your authority to decide, but I just want to remind you that you're the boss now. You're *supposed* to delegate duties."

"Point taken." He grinned. "I'm still taking the lead."

Melody chuckled. "You got it. Do we need to assign protection to her?"

A twinge of guilt pinched his nerves, but he quickly shrugged it aside. "I've got that covered."

"Going to use the local police force?"

Here goes. Explanation time. "No, I'm going to stay with her." He braced himself for the onslaught of questions.

A long pause stretched from the other end of the line.

Paul heaved a sigh. "Go ahead, I know you're holding back."

"You sure you can handle that?" Mel asked. "Last time you were around her, you were pretty taken with her, serial killer husband and all."

Damn. Nothing escaped Mel's notice. That's what made her such a good agent. "I'm taken with all the ladies, you know that."

"No, boss, this was different. You were really taken with her, not your usual love-'em-and-leave-'em style."

Paul's fingers tightened on the steering wheel. Mel hit too close to home with her observation. He had felt something back then. He'd chalked it up to pity for the beautiful bride of the Dakota Strangler. Still, he wanted to be the one to see to Elise's safety. "I was only doing what anyone would have done to help her through the trauma."

Mel chuckled. "Yeah, right. Whatever you say, boss. And she's agreed to this plan?"

Paul's lips firmed into a straight line. "Not yet. But she will. I'm on my way to the Bexar County coroner's office."

"I'll meet you there as soon as I get those calls started."

"Good deal." He ended the call, dropped the cell phone into the cup holder and pressed his foot to the accelerator, shooting his truck out on the narrow streets of Breuer. The coroner's office in San Antonio only stayed open until five. He'd just make it if he hurried.

As he merged into the interstate traffic, his cell phone vibrated, rattling against the hard plastic cup holder. He risked a glance down at the screen.

Cain.

Great. What did he want?

Paul answered the call, "Fletcher."

"Did you hear about the body they found in Breuer?" Cain asked.

"Yes." Paul held his hand steady, not in any mood to talk with Cain, but unwilling to show his hand. "Are you finished with that stack of background checks?"

"I've made some headway. I just wondered if you wanted me to look into the Breuer case."

"Not yet. It's a local issue at this point. Until the local officials invite us in, it's in their ballpark. We have no jurisdiction."

"Right. But we could offer our services. Up to them to refuse."

Paul squashed his irritation. The man really was hungry for something interesting. "Not yet. Tell you what, why don't you get with Alvarez on the government fraud case. I'll call and let him know you'll be assisting."

"I'd rather help out with the Breuer case."

"Not on your radar, Cain." So, his voice was a little too sharp. Cain was starting to get on his nerves.

"Yes, sir," Cain answered, his own response prickly.

"We'll talk in the morning when I get to the office." Paul could swear he heard muttered curses, but he couldn't be sure as a tractor-trailer rig chose that moment to roar past him on the interstate.

"Roger." Cain clicked off.

He'd been giving Cain the benefit of the doubt since he'd arrived in the San Antonio office. But if his attitude toward his new boss didn't improve soon, Cain would have to be dealt with. Either they'd get their differences out in the open and start over, or Paul would recommend a transfer for Agent Cain.

In the meantime, he had a case to work, even though he wasn't supposed to be working on it. First stop, the Bexar County Coroner.

He pulled into the coroner's office five minutes to five. Thankfully, the front door was still open. Paul stepped inside, quickly flashed his credentials at the receptionist and asked to speak to the coroner.

After the receptionist told him where he could find the coroner, Paul made his way back to the examination room, where he met Gordon Smithson, Medical Examiner for the county.

He held out his hand. "Dr. Smithson, I'm Agent Fletcher."

The doctor held up his gloved hands. "Agent Fletcher, glad you made it. I'd shake your hand, but I was just finishing up my examination of the body." He nodded toward the woman lying on the table.

Paul jammed his hands into his back pockets to keep from touching anything and tried to ignore the scent of decaying bodies and formaldehyde permeating the room. "Is this Alice Lauren Pendley?"

The door opened behind him. Mel entered and closed the distance between them. "Sorry I'm late," she said, then turned a smile toward the coroner. "Special Agent Bradley."

Smithson returned her smile, showing more animation than when Paul had introduced himself. Mel had that effect on most men. She was engaging without trying. Someone others automatically wanted to confide in.

"Do we have a cause of death?" she asked, her gaze shifting from Dr. Smithson to the body stretched out on the examination table.

Smithson's attention reverted to the victim. "Asphyxiation. Most probably, someone came at her from behind and hooked an arm around her neck. She put up a fight. See the way her fingernails are broken off? She was found naked with an Ethernet cable securing her hands behind her back and tied around her ankles. But she was dead before he bound her."

"Isn't that overkill?" Mel said.

Paul cringed at her poor choice of words, but the killer had made his point. He was either Stan Klaus or a copycat. Newspapers around the country had printed stories detailing the Dakota Strangler's methods. A book on serial killers had an entire chapter dedicated to him. Anyone with a sick mind could copy his methods.

What they shouldn't be able to do was find his wife, Alice Klaus.

Unless one of the children had unintentionally let the secret leak out. Brandon was old enough to remember his real last name. Luke had been three when his father disappeared; he probably didn't even remember the man.

Paul made a mental note to ask Brandon. Not that

he expected the boy to open up to him. For some reason, Brandon viewed Paul as a threat to his mother.

Paul had little experience with children, but how hard could it be to get the boy to warm up to him? He'd just turn up the old Fletcher charm, as Mel called it. After his visit with the coroner, he'd stop by his apartment and pack an overnight bag.

He wasn't taking no for an answer from Elise. She needed protection. Whether the killer was Stan or a copycat, he definitely had something in mind for Elise Johnson.

CHAPTER 5

Elise threw herself into the normal routine of homework with the boys, grading papers and then fixing dinner for her small family. The work should have helped her to calm down after Paul's revelation and pending return.

But she couldn't help what her mind kept conjuring. A woman floating in the Guadalupe, blond hair streaming out beside her, hands and feet tied in Ethernet cable. Every time the image surfaced, a cool chill she couldn't attribute to the new air-conditioning shook Elise's body.

When she finally dropped into her chair at the dinner table to eat the boys' favorite, mac and cheese, her shoulders were stiff and her appetite nonexistent. She forced a smile, determined to act like normal. "How was your day, Luke?"

Luke gave her a cheesy grin and spoke around the

food in his mouth. "I got four stars today for helping clean the classroom."

"Very good, Luke. I'm sure Mrs. Dobratka was impressed with your thoughtfulness."

He nodded, stuffing another heaping forkful of orangey macaroni into his mouth, half of it falling back to his plate.

"Smaller bites, big guy." Elise turned to Brandon. He'd been quiet since he'd gotten off the bus, following her around the small house, if not physically, then with his penetrating gaze. Sometimes, she thought he could see more into situations than an eight-year-old should.

"How about you, Brandon? How was your day? Did Ms. Tingle give you a spelling test today?" She placed a small bite in her mouth and pretended enjoyment.

Her oldest son set his fork beside his plate and gave her a narrow stare. "Why was that man here again?"

Glad for the little bit of food in her mouth, Elise chewed slowly before answering. "Paul is an old friend. He didn't know we lived here until yesterday. I guess he just wanted to come visit."

Brandon lifted his fork and stabbed at the food on his plate. "I don't like him."

"Why?"

"He made you cry." The boy's brows drew together in a fierce frown.

It was times like these when he looked most like his father. Elise prayed that he wouldn't take after the man. "I told you, I cried because I was happy to see him." This was only a partial lie. She had cried because she was scared out of her mind, but she'd been delighted to see Paul when he'd shown up yesterday. Maybe a little too glad. He'd been her pillar of strength when she'd really needed him. He was a man any girl could easily fall in love with. Any girl but her. She couldn't trust her instincts.

"Isn't he the man from where we used to live?"

Brandon's words broke into Elise's thoughts, and she set her fork down, fighting back a jolt of nervous tension. Since they'd left North Dakota, she hadn't talked with the boys about anything that had happened. She'd only told them that their father had died and that they were going to start a new life with new names.

Brandon hadn't asked questions at the time. If Elise wasn't mistaken, her oldest son seemed relieved that he didn't have to suffer his father's abuse. The man had leaned toward obsessive-compulsive behavior in the way he'd demanded perfection from his boys. They hadn't been allowed to run and play in their own home. Once free of his father, Brandon had taken a long time to loosen up and remember that he was a kid.

Looking at the young man across from her, Elise recognized the same little boy who'd sat straight in his chair while his father blasted him for dropping his fork on the floor.

Elise had tried to interfere with the harsh lectures once and had her face slapped so hard she'd hit the wall behind her. Every time she stepped in the middle, their punishment became harsher, and Brandon became more resentful.

How much did Brandon remember? And how much talk had he overheard when they'd been in the evacuation shelter? Did he know his father had been a killer?

"Yes. We knew Paul from where we used to live." She hoped his questions would end there. "Want some more?" Elise jumped to her feet and grabbed the pan from the stove.

"Did he know our father?" Brandon asked. "Was he his friend?"

Elise's hand shook and she set the pan back on the stove before she dropped it. "No, Brandon. He didn't know your father and he wasn't his friend."

Brandon sat staring at his food for a long moment. "I don't like him."

"He only wants to make sure we're okay and take care of us."

Her son straightened in his chair. "I'm the man of the house. I'll take care of us. I promised, remember?"

Elise dropped to a crouch next to his chair and pulled him into her arms. "Yes, sweetheart. You are the man of the house. It's just that sometimes we need a little more help around here."

"No, we don't." Brandon pushed her away, his lips set in a stubborn line.

As much as she wanted to agree with Brandon, the more Elise thought about it, the more she felt she needed Paul around. If Stan really was alive, he'd be coming after her and the boys any minute. She might as well prepare the boys for Paul's "visit" before he showed up with his suitcase. "Brandon, you're the man of the house; however, Mr. Fletcher offered to stay with us for a few days. I hope you'll be nice to him and treat him as a guest."

"We don't need him around here." Brandon pushed his chair away from the table. "We don't need anyone. I'll take care of you." He stood straight, his fists clenched beside him.

Tears threatened to well in Elise's eyes, but she refused to let Brandon see them and willed them away, though her eyes burned with the effort. "I know you will, honey. But Paul-Mr. Fletcher..." What? What could she say to convince Brandon that it was all right for Paul to stay several nights at their house? Then, a thought surfaced. "He's going to help us build a fence in the backyard."

"We already have a fence," Brandon argued.

"A different fence, one that doesn't have big gaps in it."

"So, we can get a dog?" Luke jumped out of his

chair and ran around the kitchen table, whooping. "We're going to get a dog!"

Brandon glared at his brother. "A dog?" His glare transferred to his mother. "They make a mess."

God, that was his father talking. Stan hadn't let the boys have a dog, claiming they were filthy. He had to have everything in perfect order.

Elise let a smile spill across her face. A little bit of revenge filling her veins. She didn't know why she hadn't thought about it until now. Maybe she'd taken a little too long to loosen up after being released from Stan's controlling ways. "Yes, Brandon. But not a dog. A puppy."

"A puppy!" Luke ran to his mother and threw his arms around her neck. "I'm gonna tell George. We're getting a puppy." He raced for the back door. Before Elise could stop him, he was outside, the screen slamming back in place.

"Luke!" His words sank in, and she turned to Brandon. "Who's George?"

Brandon shrugged. "I don't know."

Elise hurried to the back door and watched as Luke ran to the back corner of the yard, where the picket fence was overgrown with bushes and bramble.

The little guy yelled, "George! Guess what?"

Who was George? Elise strained to see through the overgrown hedges to the house on the other side but could only make out the roofline. For that matter, she didn't know any of her neighbors. She'd been so busy moving in, getting the boys settled in school, and setting up her own classroom that she hadn't taken the time to stroll down the block. Elise made a mental note to get to know her neighbors. For all she knew, Stan could be one of them. Another chill shook her from head to toe.

Luke yelled again and again. When no one seemed to respond, he ran back to the house. "Can I tell Kenny? Can I, Mom?"

A stab of fear lanced through her. Kendall lived a block away over the top of a slight rise in Highland Street, just enough of a rise you couldn't see her house from theirs. Luke and Brandon had been there once when Kendall had taken them there to see her Sheltie. They knew where it was. Would they try to go there on their own? Elise squatted next to her youngest son. "You're not to go to her house without me. Do you understand?"

Luke's eyes widened, his gaze going from his mother to where her hands pinched his arms. "I promise."

Elise's gaze followed his to where her hands clenched around his thin upper arms. She immediately let go, her fingers burning. Memories of Stan manhandling her ripping through her memories. "I'm sorry. I just don't want you or Brandon leaving the house without me."

"Even to play in the yard?" Brandon asked, stepping up beside his brother.

"Yes." She couldn't look into her oldest son's eyes. She didn't want him to see the fear in hers. "Just for a few days, anyway."

"Is it because of him?" Brandon persisted. "The man from North Dakota?"

Elise's heart skipped several beats before she realized Brandon was talking about Paul, not his father. "No. Not at all. Agent Fletcher is just coming to help build the fence in the backyard." Speaking of which, she'd have to come up with funds to buy the materials. Maybe she could open an account with the local hardware store until she could afford to pay it off. "Right now, why don't we go out in the backyard and see what needs to be cleaned up to get started."

Anything to get Brandon's mind off Paul until the man showed up at his door. She'd deal with his attitude then. At least Luke was on board. It didn't take much to get Luke excited. Especially with the promise of a puppy.

"Can we get our puppy today?" Luke asked, bounding down the back steps into the overgrown grass.

"Not today. We need a fence that will hold him before we can bring one home." The more she thought about it, the more she liked the idea of having a dog. A lone woman with two small children to protect could always use a dog. She'd make sure it grew into a big dog, one that protected her boys. Paul could help her find just the right breed.

As she wandered around the yard, picking up sticks and toys, she kept a close eye on the boys. The skin on the back of her neck prickled as though someone was watching her. Twice, she spun around, sure someone would be there.

No one was.

At this rate, she'd be a nervous wreck before Paul returned at sundown.

* * *

AFTER LEAVING the coroner and Mel, Paul swung by the office. Only a few agents remained at their desks. Paul breathed a sigh when he walked by Cain's empty desk. At least he didn't have to confront the man and his attitude. He wanted to place a few calls and then get back to Breuer before nightfall.

Paul stepped into his office and jerked to a halt.

Agent Cain leaped from Paul's chair, ruddy red color filling his cheeks. "Sorry. Always wondered what it was like from the other side of this desk."

"Well, now you know." Paul tamped down the anger that flared inside. "Just don't make it a habit."

"I won't." He hurried around the desk and then danced around Paul, giving him enough room to take his seat.

The seat was warm. How long had Cain been

sitting there? A new file lay square in the middle of his desk. Paul's gaze panned the files and paperwork he'd neatly stacked on his desk. Had anything moved? Had Cain been snooping through his work? The next time he left his office, Paul would be sure to lock it.

Agent Cain dropped into the cracked leather seat across from Paul and leaned back, pressing his fingertips together in a steeple. "I hope you don't mind, but after I met Alvarez on the fraud case I did some research on similar murders as the one in Breuer."

"It's not in our jurisdiction." Paul fished for a pencil from his desk drawer and then stared across at the man.

"I know," Cain said, "but it should be."

Paul's fingers tightened around his pen. "Stay out of it, Cain. It's not your case to work." He didn't trust the man yet. Especially with a case as sensitive as Elise's.

"But there are several serial murder cases it could be related to. Cases where the killer was never found."

The man didn't give up, and Paul was past being patient with him. With anger sizzling just beneath the surface of his control, Paul leaned forward. "Agent Cain, what part of 'it's not your case' did you fail to understand?"

The other agent leaned forward. "But I think we might have a serial killer in Breuer. Don't you care?"

Paul stood up so fast his chair rolled back and hit the wall. "You are not to go near Breuer. You are not to contact anyone concerning the murder. And you are not to bring up this subject again with me or anyone else. Is that understood?"

Cain shot to his feet, his face stained a mottled red, his nostrils flaring. "But..."

Rounding his desk, Paul came to a halt in front of Cain, nose-to-nose. "Do you have a problem following orders, Agent Cain?"

"No, sir." Right answer, wrong inflection, the man's contempt evident.

But Paul accepted it. "Next time I have to remind you of your orders, I'll write you up."

Cain straightened, his lips drawn into a thin line, his eyes burning with hatred. "Yes, sir."

"Dismissed."

Special Agent Cain spun on his heels and marched out the door, slamming it behind him with enough force to shake Paul's framed college diploma from the wall. It fell to the floor with a crash, the glass front shattering into a million shards.

Damn. If Cain didn't suspect Paul's involvement in the murder case before, he sure as hell would by now. So be it. He'd been warned.

Paul made a call to Elise's sister's home in Minneapolis.

His friend and former partner, Nick Tarver, answered. "Hello."

"Hey, Nick. How's the weather up there?"

"Getting darned cold." He laughed. "I hear you're having a warm fall. I could use a little of that about now."

Nick was an excellent FBI Special Agent who was always there when Paul needed help. And he needed it now. "I need a favor."

"Shoot."

"Can you check if anyone has accessed Alice Klaus's files? If anyone in the system knows what she changed her name to?"

"What's happening?"

"Found a body this morning in Breuer."

"Alice?"

"No, but whoever killed her wanted it to look like Stan Klaus. And the victim's first name was Alice."

"Damn. Brenna won't be happy about that. She'll want to hop the first plane south."

"No. Don't let her. Not in her condition." At eight months pregnant, she'd be more of a hindrance than a help to him. "Mel and I are handling it from here. If you could dig around and see if her files have been accessed, that would help."

"You got it. If you need more help, I'll come. All you have to do is say so."

"I know." Paul allowed a tight smile to stretch across his lips. Nick was one of his true friends. A man he could count on when he needed a hand. But this was his command. He had to handle things on his own. "Thanks."

He hung up, grabbed the spare shaving kit he kept in his desk drawer for the times he worked through the night and headed out the door.

A bad feeling crept across his skin, raising gooseflesh across his forearm. His footsteps quickened, urging him faster. Once he reached the parking lot, he broke into a run.

CHAPTER 6

THE SUN DIPPED below the horizon, the last lingering hints of daylight glowing a dull gray, casting the world in deep shadows. Not quite dark, but hard to see, nonetheless. Paul parked in Elise's driveway and climbed down from his truck. Rustling and voices sounded from the back corner of Elise's house, making the hairs on his arms prickle.

Though it could be a cat mewing for his supper, Paul didn't want to take the chance that it might be something else. He vaulted over the picket fence, landing softly in the grass. Slipping into the shadows beside the house, he hurried in the direction of the sound. A small dark form hovered near the very back of the lot, leaning into the bushes.

A giggle sounded like that of a child.

"Luke?" Paul called out.

A gasp was followed by the rustle of leaves in the

bushes between the back of Elise's property and the house behind it.

The little boy raced for the back door, his small feet making little sound in the grass. The rustling on the other side of the bushes faded and disappeared in the opposite direction.

Luke had his hand on the door handle when Paul caught him by the collar of his pajamas.

"Let me go!" Luke's arms flailed, his feet hammering against Paul's shins.

Paul chuckled. "It's okay, it's just me. Paul Fletcher."

Luke continued his frenzied effort to free himself. "Let me go or Mom will be mad."

The back porch light blinked on, and the door swung open. "Luke!" Elise stood in a silk robe, her hair twisted up in a towel, her eyes brilliant blue saucers in her pale face. "Paul!" The older child stood behind her, his eyes round and anxious.

"Did you lose this?" He smiled, hoping to wipe some of the fear off her pretty face.

She opened the screen and folded her son into her arms. "Luke, baby, don't ever scare me like that again!"

Brandon stared up at Paul over his mother's shoulder, his gaze narrow, unfriendly.

Paul had his work cut out for him. The boy didn't trust him. It was his job to figure out why and turn him around. The child's life could depend on it.

"Mom, I had to tell George about the puppy." Luke struggled against his mother's hold.

Elise loosened her arms enough to look into his face without letting go. "I told you, you couldn't go out in the yard without me anymore."

"But George is my friend," Luke wailed.

"I don't even know George." Her eyes narrowed and her forehead creased into fine lines Paul wanted to smooth away. "Until I meet him and talk to his mother, you aren't to talk to him again. Do you understand?"

Luke's face pinched into a frown. He pushed away from his mother's arms. "Mom! George is my friend!"

Paul stood on the back steps, feeling the boy's pain but understanding the danger involved. "Your mother is right. We need to meet George and his parents before you play with him." How could he keep the little guy from playing in his own yard without telling him that a really nasty bad guy might steal him away? The boy would have night terrors for the rest of his life.

As if just remembering who Paul was, Luke glanced up at him, his frown turning upside down into a face-splitting grin. "Are you really going to build a fence for our puppy?" His hand slipped into Paul's, and he pulled him through the door into the kitchen.

Broadsided by Luke's question, Paul allowed himself to be led to the kitchen table.

Brandon backed away, not having uttered a single word thus far.

"What's this about a fence?" Paul asked.

Elise's mouth twisted. "Sorry, I'll explain in a minute." She leaned down to her son. "Go wash the dirt off your feet and get to bed. It's way past your bedtime."

"But—"

"No buts. Go." She stood with her arms crossed over her chest, her face set in stern lines. The entire effect was muted by her soft pink robe and makeup-free face. If Paul wasn't mistaken, her lips twitched at the corners.

Luke's body drooped so much even the faces of the cartoon cars on his pajamas appeared dejected. "I want our puppy now."

"We can't get one until we get the fence up and that isn't going to be tonight. Go on." Elise swatted at the little boy's bottom, urging him toward the hallway leading to the bedrooms.

Brandon stood at a distance, his body stiff and unmoving.

"You, too, Brandon. You have school tomorrow and need to get some sleep."

Brandon shook his head. "*I'm* the man of the house. I shouldn't have a bedtime." He glared at Paul as if daring him to disagree.

So that was it. Brandon was feeling threatened by a new man in the house. That explained the immediate animosity toward him. How to fix it? Paul hadn't a clue, not having dealt with children before.

"Part of being the man of the house is knowing when to do as you're told." Elise didn't talk down to him as though he was a baby. She spoke to him like any other adult, presenting the facts without discouraging the boy. "Paul—Agent Fletcher and I need to talk about...the fence."

When Brandon still didn't move, Elise tipped her head slightly. "I'll be just fine and I'm not going anywhere. Now go to bed, please."

Brandon sighed and turned toward his bedroom. As he passed through his door, his glance shot toward Paul, his eyes narrowing. Then he disappeared.

"And close the door," Elise called out.

The door closed with a soft snick.

Elise sighed and pulled the towel off her head. Long strands of damp hair dropped to her shoulders. "I'm sorry. I meant to be more prepared for when you got here." She buried her fingers in the lengths and shook them, the scent of strawberries filling the air around him. "When I couldn't find Luke, I swear I almost had a heart attack."

With Elise standing so close in little more than a silk, calf-length robe, the teasing scent of her shampoo wrapping around his senses, Paul fought to concentrate on her words. "You don't have to 'be prepared' for me. I'm here to make sure you and the boys are all right."

"I know, but still..." Her hand waved vaguely, and she stared around at the clutter of toys littering the otherwise neat living room. Tears filled her eyes, and she sniffed, a pathetic whimper like a dog who'd been abused.

The hint of tears glazing her cornflower-blue eyes was his undoing. "A little mess never hurt anyone." Paul gave up the fight and grabbed her hand, pulling her into his arms.

She stood stiff at first, then her fingers clutched at his shirt, and she leaned into him. "I'm so scared, I don't know what to do."

"That's why I'm here. We'll figure this thing out and you can get back to your normal life."

"I don't think my life will ever be normal." She sniffed and leaned back, tears staining her cheeks. "How can it be when you're the wife of a serial killer?"

Paul didn't have an answer for her, not when all he wanted to do was kiss the tears from her cheeks. Now wasn't the time to take advantage of Elise. She was vulnerable, scared and likely to cling to anyone. But those eyes, the full, trembling lips...

Before he could think through another thought, Paul's head tipped forward.

Elise's eyes widened briefly, then she stretched

upward on her toes, her eyelids sinking to half-mast, her lips rising to meet his.

He might have pulled back at the last minute if she hadn't met him halfway. Like kinetic energy unleashed, he couldn't stop himself once he'd committed to kissing Elise Johnson. The scent of strawberries wafted around him, lured him into a deeper embrace, his hands resting on her lower back, pulled her against him. If she didn't know she'd aroused him before, she'd surely guess it now.

Instead of backing away, Elise's hands climbed up to his shoulders, lacing into the hair at his nape.

His lips slanted over hers, his tongue pushing past her teeth to taste the sweet depths of her mouth. Mint toothpaste tingled against his tongue, dragging him deeper. His hand slid up her back, the silk of her robe like a promise of the smoothness of the skin beneath, her damp hair evoking images of her naked in the shower.

He wanted more. He wanted to swing her up into his arms and carry her to her bed where he'd make sweet love to her, pushing aside all her worries, if only for a moment.

Elise gasped against his mouth, planted her hands against his chest and pushed him away.

All too soon, the fantasy ended.

He let go, shocked at his own loss of control.

Elise staggered backward, her knuckles skimming

across swollen lips. The front of her robe hung open, giving Paul a peek of one fully rounded, naked breast.

He groaned, battling the urge to pursue her and take more of what he'd just tasted. Clenching his hands into fists to keep from reaching out to her, he nodded. "I'm sorry. I shouldn't have done that." He kept his voice low so as not to disturb the boys.

Her eyes, round and blue, stared at him for a long moment, like a deer caught in the path of a predator. Then she turned away, gathering the lapels of her robe close around her. "No, I'm sorry. It wouldn't have happened if I'd been stronger. I'm such a wimp." She laughed softly with no hint of mirth reflected in the sound.

His arms rose to pull her back against him, but dropped to his side before he could follow through. "You're not a wimp. You're a worried mother. And rightly so."

"Rightly so?" She spun to face him. "Tell me something new. Did you find out who's doing this? Is it Stan?"

The hopeful look on her face made him want to tell her they'd nailed the bad guy. "We don't know much more than before."

"Stan killed five women before you caught up with him in North Dakota. Please tell me he won't kill five more before they find him this time."

"We can only do the best we can. We haven't got much to go on. It's not even in the FBI's jurisdiction, yet. Look, I'll check on this George kid and his parents for you. And I'm meeting with the sheriff tomorrow to offer our assistance in the case."

"He has to let you help. You and Mel are the only ones who understand what Stan is capable of."

"Elise, we don't know that it's Stan. The killer could be a copycat."

"But he wrote the note to *me*!" she beseeched in a hushed whisper. "How do you explain that?"

He couldn't. "Honestly, that's what has me worried."

She snorted. "You and me both. Only a few people were supposed to know of my whereabouts and name change. How does someone get that information?"

"I have your brother-in-law working on that." It wasn't much, but between Mel's hospital search and Nick's check on her file, those were the only leads they had to go on. Tomorrow, he'd meet with the sheriff and get on the inside of the case. "Look, Elise, it's getting late. You might as well turn in and get some rest."

Her answering chuckle ended in a choked sob. For a moment, she stared at the ground, her fingers clenching and unclenching. Then she straightened and looked him square in the eye. "I'm tired of being scared."

"I know."

How could he know? She'd been the one targeted

with the note. Someone had walked right into the school and stuck it in her cubby. She couldn't have the police checking at the school or her cover would be blown.

Paul stared across at her, his brows dipping low. "You're not planning on doing something crazy, are you?"

Her gaze slipped to the side and downward. "No."

"Good, because I can't be with you all the time. I need to know you're not going to go off anywhere and investigate on your own."

"I'm going to school and home."

"If you want me to, I can come into the school and ask around about the note."

Her gaze shot back to him. "No!" Heat rose up her neck and spread across her cheekbones. She pressed her palms to her face. "I don't want the principal or the other teachers to suspect anything. I want a chance to live here in peace. No one can know about my past."

Paul sighed. "Sure makes it hard to follow up on that note."

"I know," she said. "But that's the way it has to be."

"You might as well hit the sack." Paul rolled his shoulders. "Mind if I look around before calling it a night?"

She dipped her head. "Please do. I've checked that all the windows and doors are secure, but it wouldn't hurt to double-check."

"Exactly. Plus, I want to look for other vulnerable areas."

A shiver shook the woman, standing there in her robe, reminding Paul that Elise was practically naked in front of a virtual stranger. Though somehow, he didn't consider them strangers even though they'd only been in each other's company no more times than he could count on one hand.

His lips were still warm from the kiss they'd shared. When he glanced down, he realized Elise's nipples were poking out against the thin silk of her robe, the turgid peaks glaringly obvious.

She wasn't immune to his presence. Nor was she unfazed by his kiss, but he didn't need to take advantage of the fact.

Elise's cheeks blossomed with color, she crossed her arms over the evidence and ducked her head, refusing to meet his gaze. "I'll go to bed now."

"I take it I can have the couch?"

"Oh, right, yes. I'll get you a blanket." She hurried toward the cabinet in the hallway.

As her hand reached upward to open the upper cabinet door, Paul's hand caught hers. "Here, let me get it. You know you don't have to wait on me."

Her heat radiated warmth through the silk clinging to her skin. Although he wasn't touching her, he could sense the soft curves of her body only a breath away. All she had to do was lean back and he'd take her into his arms.

Unable to stop, his hand slid down her raised arm, his fingers brushing against the curve of her breast. "You feel it, don't you?" His body ached for hers, heat pooling in his groin, begging for release.

Elise sucked in a breath, her body stiffened. When she turned, she rested a hand on his chest and stared up into his eyes.

Before Paul could gather her into his arms, a door opened behind them.

Paul backed away, his hands coming away with a blanket and a pillow from the top shelf.

Elise ducked beneath his arm and confronted her oldest son.

"Mom?" Although he spoke to his mother, Brandon stared up at Paul. "Something made a noise outside my window. I'm scared."

Immediately on alert, all thoughts of making love with the beautiful Elise flew from his mind. What had he been thinking anyway? He was there to protect Elise, not force himself on her.

Paul headed for the door, determined to focus on the security he was there to provide.

CHAPTER 7

Paul spent the night on the couch, getting up every hour to go outside and check the perimeter. The noise Brandon had heard had been the branch of a mountain laurel pushed into the glass by a steadily increasing northerly breeze. Indian summer had come to an end in Breuer, the temperature plummeting thirty degrees overnight.

Before five o'clock, Paul headed out. The gray light of dawn edged the darkness out of the sky as he headed southeast into San Antonio. Rather than wake the woman he'd almost made love to last night, he'd left a note on the table telling her he'd be back that evening and for her not to go anywhere without letting him know first. He'd scribbled his cell phone number at the bottom of the note.

First stop, his apartment on the northwest side of

town, for a quick shower, shave and clean clothing. The office would be practically empty at six-thirty. Most agents didn't arrive until closer to seven-thirty or eight if they weren't out working a case. He liked the early hours all to himself without interruptions. Paperwork was hard enough to wade through on a good day.

As he started to walk out the front door of his apartment, he noticed that he had two messages on his voicemail.

He punched the play button. The first message was a call from a telemarketer wanting his mortgage business. Irritation made him hit the skip button harder than necessary. The second call started with dead air.

Paul sighed, his hand halfway to the skip button, when a disembodied voice rumbled from the machine. "Stay away from the teacher if you know what's good for you."

His heart skipped a beat, then kicked back into high gear, adrenaline shooting through his veins. He replayed the message again and again. The voice was so garbled, he couldn't recognize it. He left his apartment and headed for the office, hitting the number on his cell phone for Brian Thomas, the district's techno guru. Between the recording and the cell phone records, maybe they'd get a new lead on the killer before he took another life.

He managed to get into the office, meet with

Brian, complete some pressing paperwork and leave without being interrupted more than ten times before eight-thirty. Mel had headed for Breuer first thing that morning to question the victim's family. Cain had his head down for once, working the mound of background checks.

Paul avoided the man, not in the mood for another pissing contest on Cain's assignment. He had a date to keep with the sheriff of Kendall County and just enough time to get there, if he hurried.

* * *

BEFORE ELISE HAD the chance to set her purse in her desk drawer at school, Gerri Finch marched into her room, towing an already frazzled Principal Ford behind her.

"Ms. Johnson, I've spoken to the principal concerning your behavior toward my daughter and she agrees you're picking on her."

"No, Mrs. Finch, I did not agree." Principal Ford gave Elise a tight smile. "I agreed to listen to both sides of the story and that's all."

"Ashley has the right to free speech just like anyone else in the United States of America. It says so in the Declaration."

"The Constitution, Mrs. Finch," Principal Ford corrected. "Everyone has the right to free speech, but we have classroom rules to maintain order so that all students can learn. And these rules are what the students and the parents all agree to at the beginning of the school year."

"I don't remember agreeing to any rules." Gerri Finch tapped her alligator skin stilettos against the shiny linoleum tiles, making an angry staccato sound that beat in rhythm with the headache pounding against Elise's temples.

Principal Ford sighed. "When you signed the signature sheet at the back of the student handbook, you agreed to the rules contained within."

"Well, if I'd known it had such stupid rules in it, I wouldn't have signed it."

"Nevertheless, you did, and you and your child are bound by the rules."

Elise fought back the smile of gratitude. At least one person was on her side this morning.

"We'll see about that. Anyway, it goes, Ms. Johnson is picking on my daughter."

The principal turned to Elise.

"Ashley likes to talk in class to the point she disrupts others from getting their work done," Elise explained.

"She can't help it. She's smarter than the others." Gerri's chest swelled forward. "She gets it from both sides."

"Ashley has been late to class five times."

The principal's brows rose as she turned back to Mrs. Finch. "Three tardies is enough to send her to

Saturday school. Five is two more chances than she deserved."

"But Saturday is the cheer competition. Ashley's the captain. She has to be there."

"She should have thought of that before she arrived late for class for the fifth time." The principal held the door open for Gerri. "Now, if you'll come this way, we can continue this discussion in my office and let Ms. Johnson get on with teaching her class."

Gerri Finch glared at Elise. "This isn't over. I know your game. I'll make you regret targeting my daughter with your petty vindictiveness. You'll be gone before you collect your next paycheck." The woman's voice dripped with venom, but she allowed the principal to hook an arm through her elbow and drag her away.

Elise let out the breath she'd been holding, sagging into her chair behind her desk. Wasn't it enough she had someone depositing death threats in her cubby? Did she have to put up with over-indulgent moms as well?

Her eyes narrowed on the retreating form of Gerri Finch. What did she mean by "I know your game"? Would she know about Elise's background? She shook her head. If she did, she'd have shouted it from the rooftops of the school by now and had Elise canned so fast, she wouldn't have had time to mutter the word *but*.

She shook off the thought and got down to the

business of shaping young minds with lessons from the past. If only the past wasn't prone to repeat performances.

* * *

Paul arrived at Denny's at exactly nine. His gaze panned the tables and booths for the heavyset sheriff, spying him in the far left corner.

The sheriff waved a hand toward the opposite booth seat. "I've already ordered," he said, lifting his cup of coffee toward the waitress and nodding at Paul.

Taking her cue, the young brunette hurried to the pot of coffee warming at the counter and collected a clean cup. She returned to their table and smiled at Paul. "You're new around here." She set the mug in front of him and poured steaming, fragrant coffee into it. "Need to see a menu?"

He hadn't realized just how hungry he was until she'd asked. "No, thanks. I'll have two eggs over-medium and wheat toast."

She nodded without taking down a word he spoke. "That's what I like, a man who knows what he wants."

The sheriff's chuckle followed her retreating form. "Mandy's a pretty little thing. Watch out, though. She's tough. Comes from hardy stock. Her parents own a small Angora goat ranch in the hill country near Sisterdale."

Paul's gaze followed the pretty Mandy, but his thoughts kept to a certain blonde he'd wanted more than anything to keep kissing last night. "Thanks for the recommendation. But I'm not interested." He leaned back against the slick vinyl seat and sipped his coffee. "What can you tell me about Alice Lauren Pendley?"

The sheriff's mouth pulled into a tight line. "Lauren was a good kid. Grew up here in Breuer, member of the 4-H club, graduated from University of Texas at San Antonio two years ago." He shook his head, his gaze directed toward the window. "Her parents were so proud. Neither one had ever been to college. Hardworking folks, always looking out for others. It's a damned shame. And Lauren was engaged to be married next spring."

Paul listened, waiting for the sheriff to get to the pertinent details of the murder investigation.

"Her mother called us the night before last when she didn't come home from work."

"Where did she work?"

"At the drugstore. She wanted to go to pharmacy school next fall. Had her acceptance and everything."

"Did anyone see her leave?"

"The manager walked her to her car every night. Only he was off that night. She left by herself. No one saw her get into her car."

"Is there a security camera for the parking lot?"

"Already checked it. The manager insisted the cameras were aimed at the guest parking up front and the employee parking in the rear of the building. Again, not that night. We don't know if the wind or someone with killing on his mind shifted the camera to point at the treetops, but that's all that was on the recording from eight o'clock that night until we confiscated the video at eight the next morning."

Paul leaned forward. "How do you know the shift happened at eight?"

"We watched from the time Lauren got to work until she was scheduled to leave. We could see the camera shift around eight o'clock."

"Fingerprints on the camera?"

The sheriff shook his head. "Not a one. But we found a brick close by and a dent in the camera casing. We did the math. It wasn't the wind."

"Could you trace the brick?"

"It was from the stack in Mrs. Veatch's backyard behind the drugstore." The sheriff looked up as Mandy delivered their plates.

Steam rose from the sheriff's fried bacon and sausage, sending waves of tempting aromas toward Paul. His own eggs and toast didn't seem quite as appealing as the plate of heart attack the sheriff planned to consume. "Did you review the indoor videos for customers entering and leaving around eight that night?"

"We've gone over and over the video. Neither the officers nor the store employees recognized most of the customers."

"This is a small town. Wouldn't you know a majority of the people here?" Paul took up his fork, suddenly ravenous, his stomach aching for nourishment.

"We're small, but we get a lot of transients from the interstate who come in for over-the-counter medications." The sheriff shrugged. "Short of questioning all the hotel clerks and RV park attendants about whether or not they've seen the people in that clip before, I don't have much to go on."

Paul set his cup on the table. "What about the crime scene? Did the state crime lab process it?"

"Yeah, they had a team come in and comb over the area. Because of the lack of rain, the river's way down. Heck, it's more like a creek. The girl didn't float far from where he dumped her in the water."

"Any footprints?"

"No. The guy was careful. He obviously knew to cover his tracks. The Ethernet was standard cable used by just about everyone in the industry. No tracks, no witnesses. He did it by the books, leaving no traces."

How did he catch a killer who didn't want to be caught? A man trying to make a point with Elise. He had to be in on the ground level with the sheriff's office, investigating alongside Breuer's finest to ensure no stone remained unturned. Something their less experienced eyes might miss, he might pick up on. "Do you want the FBI's help on this one?"

The sheriff stared across the table at Paul. "I don't want the FBI taking over our case, if that's what you're askin'."

Paul nodded. "Fair enough. But we might have more resources available that could help speed up the investigation."

"Look, I don't mind a little help. We're always short-handed, what with cattle getting out of fences and domestic disputes we answer to, but I don't want some yahoo muckin' around and messin' up my investigation, got that?"

"Yes, sir." Paul liked the old coot, despite his belligerence. "How about if my partner, Special Agent Bradley, and I work alongside you until we find the guy who did this?"

"Is Agent Bradley like you?"

"A little, only she fancies herself a Texan even though she grew up in Boston."

The sheriff's stern face settled into a grin. "Can't be all bad if she wants to be a Texan. Not everyone can be one, though. It's something you gotta live, breathe and defend." He nodded at Paul. "Not everyone opens up to people with funny accents."

"Like me, right?" Paul returned the sheriff's grin. "I'll work on that."

"My advice to you is to get a hat." The sheriff

nodded at his on the seat beside him. Paul was saved from a response when the sheriff's cell phone chirped, and he reached for it. "Excuse me."

Paul ate several bites of the greasy eggs, his stomach churning over the lack of evidence he could sink his teeth into.

The sheriff listened to the caller, the smile on his face fading, dipping into a fierce frown. He set his napkin beside his plate. "You tell Mrs. Holzhauer I'll be there in five minutes. Don't let anyone inside the girl's apartment until the state crime lab can get there and process the scene."

Paul couldn't feign indifference to the call. Every hackle he had stood at full attention.

When the sheriff disconnected, he stood, leaving the majority of his food untouched. "We've had another woman reported missing at the Hilltop Apartments. Ready to go to work?"

Paul rose, tossing enough cash on the table to cover the meal for both of them and a sizable tip for Mandy. "Let's go. I'll follow you."

* * *

A FEW MINUTES before the last class of Elise's day, Kendall McKenzie rushed in, followed by Alex Mendoza. "Ms. Johnson." She stopped short and let out a relieved sigh. "Oh, good, you're still here."

Elise smiled at the girl. "Of course, I'm here. We

have class at this time." She laughed. "Why would you think otherwise?"

Alex nudged Kendall in the side hard enough to take the wind out of her next words. "No reason."

It wasn't like Alex to lie about something. "No really, why wouldn't I be in my classroom?"

"Because my mother is going to have you fired." Ashley Finch flounced into the room and slung her backpack on the floor beside her desk.

Elise fought not to roll her eyes.

Students filed in and took their seats just as the tardy bell buzzed in the hallway.

Elise had a job to do, whether she felt like it or not. And she definitely didn't feel like forcing history into the closed minds of hormonal teenagers when a killer ran free in the same town. But what else would she do? Run home and hide under the bed until the danger passed?

She refused to cower. If her sister could bring criminals to justice while being personally targeted, Elise should at least be able to teach a few high school kids without running screaming.

She'd pulled out her history book and opened it to the current chapter when Caesar strolled through the door, bumped Alex out of his seat and plopped down in it.

"Hey!" Alex picked himself up off the floor and glared at Caesar. "That's my seat."

Caesar glanced down at the desk and back at Alex. "Doesn't have your name on it."

Elise inhaled, let it out and crossed her arms over her chest. "Out."

Caesar's dark brows rose into the long, unruly hair hanging down in his eyes. "Who, me?"

"Now." Elise's eyes narrowed into slits.

"And what are you going to do if I don't leave?" His mouth twisted into an irritating smirk. "Your boyfriend isn't here today."

Elise didn't bother arguing with the young man. She spun on her heel and marched to the intercom attached to the wall. Before she could punch the button, Caesar was on his feet and across the room.

His big hand clamped down over the keypad, blocking her from making the call to the office. "What are you going to do now?" he challenged.

She made a move to step around him and head for the door.

He blocked her exit, the wall of his body effectively trapping her inside the classroom.

"Very well." She glanced toward the students who watched with varying expressions on their faces. Some had wide-eyed looks, shock and fear rooting them to their seats. Her glance returned to Caesar. "Someone go get the principal...and security." She refused to show fear. Bullies like Caesar thrived on fear.

"Do it and you won't live to graduate," Caesar warned.

The classroom remained silent. No one moved toward the door.

Elise rolled her eyes. "Good grief, Caesar, what do you really think this little power game you're playing is going to buy you?"

"A little satisfaction." He flicked his finger at the vee in her blouse. "If you want a real man to keep you warm at night, you need to get rid of that boyfriend of yours. Besides, a pretty teacher like you shouldn't be sleeping around. Word gets out to the school board, and you might not have a job anymore."

Her frown deepened. "What do you know about..." She clamped her teeth down on her bottom lip. Had he been spying on her? Hanging around her house? She'd assumed Caesar was relatively harmless for the most part. As the class bully, he pushed people around, but she hadn't heard of him breaking any laws or seriously harming anyone. Would he, now that she'd made him mad?

Movement caught Elise's attention. Alex and Kendall had eased toward the door and stood poised for flight. With his back to them, Caesar couldn't see them slide out and race down the hall toward the administrative offices.

"Hey-" Ashley began.

"Caesar, what's this really about?" Elise asked, desperate to keep Caesar's attention.

"I don't like being pushed around."

Elise snorted. "But you don't mind pushing others around. That makes a lot of sense."

"What do you know? You're a white girl in a white man's world. You don't know nothin'."

"You don't know anything," Elise corrected automatically.

"What are you, my English teacher now?"

Elise sighed. "No, but if you don't tell me what's really wrong, you'll only end up in trouble every time."

"I don't care. Why should I?" He stepped closer to her. "School's just stupid."

The hairs on her arms raised and she fought to keep from moving backward. She had to take a stand, even if she got hurt in the process. Bullies like Caesar pushed and pushed until they hit a brick wall. She meant to be his brick wall.

"Well, you're not scaring me, Caesar. You need to leave the class and let me get on with teaching the people who want to make something of their lives."

He jerked his head toward the others. "You think history is going to get them out of this town?"

"Maybe not directly, but it might help them to make better decisions, like when to pick a fight and when not to."

Footsteps echoed from the hallway. Officer West, the Breuer police officer assigned to the high school,

Principal Ford and a couple of the bigger coaches hurried toward Elise's classroom.

Caesar glanced over his shoulder and snorted. "You got lucky, teach." He faced her, his eyes narrowing. "This time. You won't always." Then he vaulted across a desk, opened a window to the outside and jumped through.

The police officer burst through the door.

Elise pointed at the open window. Caesar had dropped to the ground and taken off running.

The officer followed Caesar out the window, his belt catching on the metal window frame, slowing him down.

Students erupted into chatter. Principal Ford dismissed all but one of the coaches while Elise collapsed into her chair.

The rush of adrenaline that had kept her toe-to-toe with Caesar receded, leaving her drained.

"Ms. Johnson, Elise?" The principal leaned over her. "Why don't you and I take a break. Coach Ueker will sit with your class."

Great. Three times in the past two days her abilities as a teacher responsible for a classroom of teenagers had been in question. Was Principal Ford about to fire her? If so, what would she do for a job? How would she pay the mortgage?

"Principal Ford, Ms. Johnson didn't do anything to make Caesar mad." Bless Alex. The kid might be half the size of Caesar, but he had a heart.

"It's okay, Alex. I'll explain what happened to Principal Ford. Everyone, open your books to page..." She stared at her desk and the book lying open where she'd intended to begin the class lecture. "Page 242. I want you to start reading there and answer the questions in the back of the chapter. I'll be back shortly." She hoped.

Elise stood, her legs shaking beneath her, and followed the principal to her office.

CHAPTER 8

Paul accompanied the sheriff to the apartment.

The Hilltop Apartments manager, Mrs. Holzhauer, stood at the open door to Mary Alice Fenton's second-floor apartment, clutching a folded paper in her hand. "I didn't touch anything, just like you said. Well, except when I went inside to ask why Miss Fenton left her door open. The place was a mess, but Miss Fenton wasn't home. If the door hadn't been standing wide open, I wouldn't have thought anything of it." The older woman sucked in a breath and let it out. "I called her work number, and they said she didn't report to work this morning. They left a message on her voice mail, but she didn't call back."

"You did all the right things, Mrs. Holzhauer." Sheriff Engel patted the woman's shoulder.

She wrung her hands, her narrow frame clad in a

gray polyester pantsuit looked as gray as the overcast sky. "I saw the local news. I know they found a woman murdered just yesterday, but they haven't released her name. I just wondered..."

Paul hung back and let the sheriff take the lead.

"It wasn't Mary Alice, Mrs. Holzhauer." Sheriff Engel took a notebook out of his pocket. "Do you have Miss Fenton's cell phone number?"

"It's not on her application, just her work number." Mrs. Holzhauer stared at the paper in her hand. "I know she has a cell phone because I saw her talking on one when she drove out of here yesterday morning to go to work."

The sheriff leaned over Mrs. Holzhauer's shoulder to look at the paper she held. "What about an emergency contact?"

Mrs. Holzhauer shoved the paper toward him. "I pulled her application from the file. The number listed is her mother's." The older woman shook her head. "It's a horrible thing to report to a mother."

The sheriff shook his head as he scanned the application. "Now, Mrs. Holzhauer, we don't know that anything untoward has happened to Mary Alice."

"I know, I know, but still..." She wrung her hands, her gaze following the sheriff through the door of the empty apartment. "You think the same guy that got the other lady might have Mary Alice?"

Paul stepped forward. "Mrs. Holzhauer, we don't know, but we'll do the best we can to find out. For now, we need to look around. Will you be all right by yourself in your office?"

Mrs. Holzhauer nodded, backing away, taking Paul's hint. "I called my sister-in-law. She said she'd come to keep me company the rest of the day if necessary. If you need anything, just ask." She hurried down the metal steps, glancing all around before she exited the building to walk across the parking lot.

Paul shook his head. It was a lousy way to live when a woman had to be afraid of walking from one building to another in broad daylight. He followed Sheriff Engel into the apartment, careful not to disturb anything that could be classified as evidence. The police officer who'd been the first on scene waited in the parking lot for the state crime lab team.

Technically, the woman hadn't been reported missing by her family, and she hadn't been missing long enough to qualify for a missing persons report. But with the discovery of a murdered woman only a day prior to Mary Alice's disappearance, the sheriff had to take action.

The small apartment had a collection of mismatched furniture, likely thrift shop specials or hand-me-downs from family members. A pair of jeans hung from the corner of a door, stretched out as if to dry. A plate with a piece of leftover pizza was on the table, the pizza only half eaten as if Mary Alice had planned to finish it.

The sheriff's gaze panned the room. "No signs of

forced entry, no signs of struggle. You see anything different?"

Paul shook his head, staring at the pizza. "She might have been eating the pizza when someone came to the door."

"With no signs of forced entry, I'd venture to guess she opened the door. The chain is still intact, so she didn't feel threatened by whoever stood on the other side."

"Someone she knew, maybe."

"Or someone she'd trust."

"What about her purse?" Paul nodded toward the black leather bag on the counter, a set of car keys lying next to it.

The sheriff used his pen to push the purse open and peered inside. "The wallet's inside."

"Cell phone?"

"No." The sheriff pulled out his own phone and hit the speed dial. "I'll get her cell phone number from her employer. I hate to think we might have a serial killer on our hands. But with one woman dead already, I'm willing to bet Mary Alice's disappearance is related."

While the sheriff placed his call to the state police, Paul worked his way around the room and into the bedroom, careful not to touch anything. The covers on the bed lay in disarray but not like a struggle had taken place. More like someone who didn't make the bed after sleeping in it. In the bathroom, cosmetics and perfume littered the counter but no sign of a cell phone.

The sheriff's voice carried to him from the other room.

When he emerged, the sheriff was hitting the off button on his cell phone.

"Not a robbery or they would have taken the purse and the car." Paul circled the living room, pausing to stare at a picture sitting on the end table beside a faded blue couch. Both people in the photo were smiling. The young man, possibly in his late twenties, and the young woman, vaguely familiar with long blond hair and blue eyes. Paul's heart plunged to his stomach, churning the food he'd eaten earlier. "This must be Mary Alice."

The sheriff moved to join Paul by the couch. "I've seen her around town. Always has a smile."

"Know the guy in this picture?"

The sheriff bent forward and stared hard at the man in the picture. "He looks like the police officer assigned to the high school."

"What?" Paul straightened, his heart leaping against his chest, pounding so hard he couldn't hear himself think.

The sheriff frowned at him. "Is there something wrong with that? I've met him once or twice at football games at the high school stadium. Last name's West." The sheriff scratched his chin. "Colton West, if I'm not mistaken. Kinda new. Only been on the city police force for two or three months."

The urge to get to the high school and find Officer Colton West hit Paul hard, but he kept his cool in front of the sheriff. He wanted to get to Elise as quickly as possible. Whoever had left Elise the note in her box had access to the school. A campus police officer had access to every place on campus, including the front office. "Let's start there. Maybe he can help us pinpoint the last time she'd been seen."

"Yeah. As soon as the state police crime scene investigators arrive, I'm on it."

"I have to make some calls to check in with the office. Want to meet up at the high school in, say an hour?"

"I'll meet you there." The sheriff returned his attention to the notebook in his hand, scribbling words on the page.

Paul left the apartment complex and pushed the posted speed limits on his way to the high school on the other side of Breuer.

At a stop light, he dialed Brian.

"Hey, Fletcher."

"Anything on that phone call?"

"Got an electronic copy of your phone records just a few minutes ago. The fastest I've ever gotten anything from the phone company. Gotta love technology."

Paul wanted to tell Brian to get to the point. The

light changed and he concentrated on making a left turn onto Main Street.

"Anyway, I scanned for the time you gave me and sure enough, there was a phone call from a cell phone. Only the cell phone was a burner, one of those disposable types you can't trace."

"Great." Another dead end and his killer was using all the tricks.

"I'm trying to trace the phone back to the dealer. Maybe we can get an ID on the person who bought it."

"Thanks, Brian." Paul hung up and resisted the urge to throw his cell phone out the window. They were running out of time on this case. Another woman could be fighting for her life as they chased dead-end clues.

The afternoon had passed, and school would be getting out soon. As he pulled into the parking lot, the boy he'd caught giving Elise hell sprinted past him. A man dressed in the solid black uniform of the Breuer Police Department pounded the pavement after the kid. The kid had a good hundred yards on the officer. Unless he was in better shape than a seventeen-year-old, he didn't stand a chance of capturing the punk.

Unfortunately, the cop chasing the kid was the one Paul wanted to talk to.

The best way to speed this up was to slow the kid down.

Paul whipped his vehicle around and raced after the punk, pulling in front of him. He spun his steering wheel hard to the left, spinning the car broadside on the road leading out of the high school campus. Paul leaped out and gave chase.

The young man changed directions and ran for the five-foot-tall, chain-link fence bordering the road. With the ease of youth, he grabbed the wire, and vaulted over the top. He dropped to the ground on the other side and disappeared between the tightly packed houses of a neighborhood.

By the time Paul could get over the fence, the kid would be long gone.

The cop skidded to a halt in front of Paul. "Give me one good reason why I shouldn't haul your butt to jail for driving like that on a school campus." He sucked in enough air to fill his lungs, his dark-eyed gaze angry.

Raising his hands, Paul smiled. "Hey, I was only trying to slow him down."

"We know where he lives. I'll catch up with him later."

Paul pulled out his FBI credentials. "FBI Special Agent Paul Fletcher."

The cop's hands slid off his hips and he relaxed a little. "Okay, that's a reason. I'm not so sure it's good enough to justify reckless driving on campus, but I'll give you the benefit of the doubt. What brings you here?"

Paul studied him. He didn't appear to be nervous about an FBI agent showing up. If he'd had anything to do with his girlfriend's disappearance, he wasn't giving any signs via body language.

"You know Mary Alice Fenton?" Paul asked.

The cop stiffened, his eyes narrowing. "Yeah, why?"

"When was the last time you saw her?"

"Last night around eleven o'clock." His eyes widened. "Is Mary okay? What's this all about?"

Paul hadn't planned to question the boyfriend until the sheriff arrived, but he was here, and the opportunity had presented itself. "Her apartment door was open this morning. The manager got concerned and called her office. She didn't show up for work today. Did she say anything to you about that?"

Officer West shoved a hand through his hair. "Jesus. No. No, she didn't say anything about missing work." He looked around. "I should go check on her."

"I just came from Miss Fenton's apartment. The Kendall County sheriff is there now, waiting for state crime scene investigators. Do you know if Miss Fenton has a cell phone?"

"Yeah, she does." Officer West pulled his cell phone out of his pocket and punched one of the numbers, his expression hopeful.

Paul waited, quietly.

After a long minute, the younger man hit the off button, his body sagging. "Her voicemail picked up."

If the cell phone had been in the apartment, the sheriff would have found it by now. But why would she leave her apartment with her cell phone and not her purse or keys?

"I really should go over to her place."

Paul shook his head. "They wouldn't let you in and she's not there." His gut told him the police officer had nothing to do with his girlfriend's disappearance, but he wasn't ruling anything out yet.

Officer West held out his hands. "What am I supposed to do? I can't do nothing."

"You can start by getting on the phone with all your mutual friends. See if anyone has seen her." Paul pulled a card out of his wallet and handed it to the officer. "If you hear anything at all, give me a call or call the sheriff."

"I will." Officer West tucked the card into his pocket and stared at the fence the young punk had jumped.

Paul would bet he wasn't seeing the kid or the fence.

The school bell rang. Paul glanced at his watch. Elise was getting off work now. He could meet her at her classroom and escort her home. First, he'd better move his car out of the middle of the road before the stampede of teenagers exited campus.

When he passed through the main entrance, Elise

was leaving the office, a tissue clutched in her hand and her eyes red-rimmed. When she spotted him, she hurried toward him.

Paul opened his arms, and she fell into them.

"Ewww, Ms. Johnson." A passing student snickered, the smirk on his face freezing when Paul glared at him.

Elise pushed Paul to arms length and then stepped away. "I'm sorry. It's just been a really bad day."

"Want to tell me about it?"

She gave him a half smile. "Later. I need to get home to my boys."

"I'll take you."

"No, I need my car. I like to have my own transportation. You can't be playing chauffeur for me. You have a job."

"You need protection."

"Yeah, that and a bucket of money." She touched his arm. "Please. I need to do things on my own. I'll be careful."

Paul didn't like letting her out of his sight, but she was right. He had work to do and so did she. As long as he provided protection at night, she ought to be okay. The two women who'd disappeared had done so after dark, as far as he could ascertain.

"Okay. I'll meet you at your place this evening. Don't open your door for anyone and keep a close eye on the boys."

"I won't and I will." She grinned. "Later?" She turned to go back to her classroom, stopped and came back to the office. "Will you do me a big favor?"

When she looked up at him with those big blue eyes, he would have walked off a cliff for her. "Anything."

"This may sound stupid, but I forgot to check my mailbox in the office." Elise remembered how the Dakota Strangler left messages every time he killed another woman. Maybe subconsciously, she'd avoided her mailbox because she didn't want to find another note. Another note meant another death.

"You want me to check it?" Paul's voice penetrated her musings.

Elise shook off the morbid worries and straightened her shoulders. "No, no. I'll do it, but will you wait until I do...just in case?"

"I'll be right here."

ELISE WALKED BACK into the administrative office, her footsteps dragging. If another note showed up in her box from whoever was tormenting her, she didn't know what she'd do.

Without looking at her box, she turned to the secretary. "Becky, did you see who put the note in my box the day before yesterday, by chance?"

The slightly plump and perky secretary tipped her head to the side. "No, I don't recall seeing who left it.

I think it might have been there before I came in that morning. Why?"

"No reason."

"Wasn't there a name on it?" Becky asked.

"No."

The secretary's eyes widened, and a smile blossomed on her face. "A secret admirer?" She clapped her hands together. "How sweet."

Elise almost burst out laughing, but she was afraid her laughter would turn to tears all too easily. "Uh, no. Not a secret admirer."

Becky's smile slipped. "Oh."

To avoid further questions, Elise braced herself and turned toward her box. An envelope lay tilted to the left.

Her hand shook as she reached for it. On the front, written in blue ink, were the words *Ms. Johnson's insurance forms*.

All the air left Elise's lungs in a rush and she dragged in more, a nervous giggle rising to the top of her throat. All that worry for nothing. Elise took another steadying breath and turned a smile toward Becky. "See you tomorrow."

"Those insurance forms are due back in the office by Friday," Becky called out.

Outside, Paul's gaze questioned her without a word being spoken.

She smiled. "Just insurance papers." Tucking the envelope inside her purse, she headed for the door, glad Paul had met her at school. Her day hadn't been the best, but with a hunky agent spending the night at her house, things were looking up.

Paul inspected her car inside and out before he opened the door for her. Elise didn't question him, but a chill slithered down her back. What if someone had tampered with it while it sat in the school parking lot overnight? She really should have brought it home yesterday. Elise shrugged. Anyone could just as easily tamper with it outside her home.

She'd had the car for two years, but getting inside it now gave her no comfort.

"I'll see you home, then I need to head to the office for a couple hours to check in."

"You don't have to babysit me, you know," Elise insisted, feeling more and more like a burden. "I hate to be such a problem."

He touched a finger to her lips, startling her into silence.

"Ms. Johnson, you are not the problem." He winked and stepped away, closing her door firmly between them.

She sat for a moment, her tongue sliding across her lips, the salty taste of his finger giving her entirely different tingles than the scary ones of earlier.

Get a grip, girl. You're not on the market. A cold slap of reality hit her. She didn't need to get involved now or ever. All her concentration should be on raising her sons and keeping them safe.

With the little pep talk firmly in mind, she shifted into Drive and blended into the line of cars filled with teens and their parents eager to get away from the school and back home.

Once off campus, she headed for Highland Street, cutting through the back roads. Paul followed.

A red light caught him. Without a good place to pull off the road, Elise continued toward home, turning left at the next intersection. She still couldn't see Paul and slowed. No one was behind her, so she slowed even more until she was almost at a standstill.

As she peered into her rearview mirror a dark object sailed into her peripheral vision. Something smashed into the front windshield. Elise screamed and flung one of her hands up to protect her face. Glass shattered, tiny shards projecting through the air. Elise slammed her foot to the break and squeezed her eyes shut.

Too late. Little slivers of glass prickled behind her eyelids. Afraid to open her eyes and unable to move, she sat frozen in her seat, her heart hammering in her chest.

CHAPTER 9

AT LEAST FIVE times in the two minutes he sat at the red light, Paul debated running it. Each time he talked himself down. What could happen to Elise in two minutes?

The light changed. Just as Paul pressed his foot to the accelerator, a young woman driving a burgundy sports car and talking on a cell phone ran the red light.

"Damn!" Paul slammed his foot on the brakes to keep from hitting the oblivious idiot. As soon as she passed, Paul checked for oncoming traffic. Nothing. He hit the accelerator and sped forward, determined to catch up with Elise before she got home.

At the next corner, he barely slowed, taking the turn a little faster than was safe for the normal driver. His tires squealed and he slowed. That's when he saw Elise's metallic gray, four-door sedan with the blue and gold Minnesota Vikings bumper sticker parked in the middle of the road.

Paul slammed his foot to the brakes and skidded to a halt behind her. He engaged his emergency blinker and jumped from his truck.

As he rounded the side of the vehicle, shards of glass on the ground caught the sunlight and twinkled up at him. Elise sat inside, her body rigid, her hands covering her face.

Paul's heart jumped into his throat, and he jerked at the door handle. "Elise!" The door was locked. "Elise, unlock the door." With desperation trumping reason, Paul yanked on the door, knowing it wouldn't open until she unlocked it.

Her eyes still shut, Elise dropped her left hand to the armrest and fumbled to locate the power switch for the door lock.

At the faint click, Paul jerked the door handle and flung open the door. "Elise?"

Both hands were covering her eyes again. "I have glass in my eyes. I'm afraid to do anything in case it cuts me."

"Just be still. I have a bottle of water in my truck. I'll be right back."

"I'm not going anywhere."

Reluctant to leave her, Paul ran back to his truck and rummaged in the backseat for the bottle of water he kept handy for after a workout. By the time he got back to her, Elise had turned sideways in her seat and set her feet on the pavement.

"Here, let me help you." He hooked an arm around her waist and helped her straighten without bumping her head. He steered her to the curb. "How bad does it hurt?"

"Just prickles like big grains of sand in my eye. But I'm afraid to blink or open my eyes until I have something to remove the glass."

When she'd straightened, Paul slid his hand from around her waist up beneath the hair at the back of her neck. "Lean back and I'll flush your eyes with the water."

She tipped her head back, a small chuckle escaping her. "You're going to smear my mascara."

That she could laugh at a time like this was more than Paul could take and not kiss her. He pressed his lips to her temple. "I promise not to laugh." Holding the bottle poised over her left eye, he said, "Tilt your head a bit to the left so we don't wash it out of one eye into the other."

Oblivious to the cars creeping around them in the street, Paul poured water over her eyelid. "Open slowly."

Elise's left eyelid fluttered open. "That's good." She eased her eyelid closed and opened it again. "Better. Now the other."

Paul repeated the routine on the other side until he emptied the bottle. "Feel like we got it all?"

"I think so. When I get home, I'll get under the shower."

"No, I'm taking you to an optometrist. You don't mess with your eyesight."

"I'll be fine. I need to get home to my sons. I promise I'll make an appointment tomorrow." Elise pushed her damp hair out of her face and crossed the pavement to examine her car. The front windshield was shattered. She wouldn't be driving it until she replaced the windshield. "What did I hit?"

Paul surveyed the car and the surrounding area. He knelt beside her back left tire, lifted a large red brick, and held it up, anger burning in his chest. "Did you see who threw it?"

Elise's face blanched. "I was looking in the rearview mirror. All I saw was a shadow of the brick when it hit."

Paul made a mental note of the street name and numbers to report to the sheriff and the wrecker service. If he knew who'd thrown the brick, he'd skip the sheriff altogether and perform a little vigilante justice himself. First, he had to get Elise home safely. "Come on. We'll pick up the boys on the way to the optometrist."

Elise shook her head, her lips twisting into a wry grin. "You really should run screaming from me. I'm beginning to think my life is jinxed." Although she smiled, her voice cracked, and she sniffed.

His heart constricting inside his chest, Paul

reached out and held her arms, staring down into watery blue eyes with black smudges beneath them where her mascara had run. He couldn't recall anyone more beautiful. "You're okay." Then he bent to brush her lips with his.

Her eyes widened and her fingers rose to touch where his lips had been. "Please don't do that again."

"I'm sorry. There's something about you that I can't seem to resist." When he bent to kiss her again, she pressed her hands against his chest, stopping him.

"Remember? I'm the wife of a serial killer."

"No, as you reminded me, you're Elise Johnson." He'd already stepped way over the line of FBI agent and protected citizen, so he held off. As much as he wanted to kiss her again, it had to be her choice.

The hands on his chest bunched in the fabric of his shirt and pulled him down until his lips met hers. "I know I'm going to regret this, but..." She pressed her lips to his, her tongue sweeping past his teeth to tangle with his.

A bright yellow school bus eased around their parked cars.

As though just remembering where she was, Elise straightened, her eyes going wide. "I must be out of my mind."

"Because you kissed me?"

"I didn't kiss you, you kissed me."

"No, sweet Elise, you kissed me."

She pressed her fingers to her lips and stared at the bus, thinking of all the reasons she shouldn't be kissing Paul and not caring about even one of them at that moment. A sea of faces peered through the glass windows of the school bus at her and the wrecked car. Among the faces, a familiar one stood out.

Brandon.

Sometimes, being a mom was tough. Especially when you wanted to be yourself. "We have to get going." She stepped out of Paul's arms and reached inside her car for her purse and the stack of papers that needed grading. "Think the car will be all right if we leave it here?"

"I'll get a wrecker to pick it up. There's plenty of room for other cars to go around in the meantime." Paul held open the passenger seat door to his truck.

Once she'd buckled herself into the leather seat, Elise scrubbed at the black under her eyes, while Paul rounded the hood of the pickup and slipped in beside her. "Do you think whoever wrote the note also threw the brick?"

Paul frowned. "No."

Elise waited for more, but it wasn't forthcoming. "No?"

"Whoever is behind the murder victim and the missing girl wouldn't be so sloppy as to throw a brick and risk being seen." Paul shifted into gear and pulled around the stranded car, picking up speed to catch the bus.

Paul placed a call to Sheriff Engel while Elise called her insurance company, each reporting the damage.

When they reached Highland Street, the bus had just pulled away from the bus stop. Brandon walked toward the house, his shoulders slumped. Luke dragged his backpack behind him by one of the loose straps.

Elise shook her head. "I can't keep that child in backpacks." Though she was talking about Luke, her heart went out to her oldest son. As soon as Luke turned and saw the truck, he let out a whoop. "It's Paul! It's Paul!"

Brandon didn't look back but continued toward the house.

Paul rolled the window down and called out to Luke. "Climb in the backseat."

"Yay! I get to ride in the monster truck!" Luke climbed up on the running board and jerked the door open. He slung his backpack onto the floorboard and clambered up into the truck. "Can we go to the rodeo? Can we?"

"Luke, honey," Elise said. "The rodeo has already come and gone. We'll have to wait until next fall when it comes back."

"Are you going to start on the fence? Can we get our puppy?"

Paul laughed out loud. "Do you ever breathe?"

"Sure. All the time." He huffed in and out and patted his chest. "See?"

Brandon reached the house before the truck pulled into the drive. He dug in a side pocket of his backpack, unearthing a key. Without glancing their way, he inserted the key in the door and pushed it open.

Paul shifted into Park, his gaze on the boy.

What would it take for Brandon to warm up to Paul? The boy had lost one parent already. He might think of Paul as someone who might take his mother away from him. How could he convince the child that would never happen?

Luke burst out of the truck and dropped to the ground. He rounded the house and ran into the backyard.

Paul glanced across at Elise. "Want me to talk to him?"

"No. I will." She sighed. "Give me a minute, will you?"

Elise gathered her purse and the papers and headed into the house.

Once inside, she dropped the papers on the counter and hurried down the hall to Brandon's room. Only he wasn't there. He'd stopped in front of Elise's room and stood just inside the doorway, staring at the wall, his eyes round, his face pale.

"Brandon?" Elise closed the distance between

them and dropped to her knees beside her son. "Baby, what's wrong?"

He didn't look at her, he just kept staring straight ahead. "I didn't do it, Mommy."

Elise's heart flipped in her chest, and she turned her head so slowly she felt she was in a time warp.

On the clean white wall over the headboard of her bed were words scrawled in bold black letters.

Roses are red
Her eyes were blue
She was a blonde
And looked just like you.

Lying below the note, neatly stretched across the snowy white pillowcase, was a lock of long blond hair.

"Elise?" Paul called out from the living room.

Elise straightened and turned Brandon away from her room. "It's okay, Brandon. I know you didn't do it."

"But who? Who would have done it?" he whispered. Then his gaze locked on Paul and his body stiffened.

Before Elise realized what was happening, Brandon flew at Paul, scratching and kicking, screaming at the top of his voice. "You did it! It's all your fault! You never should have come!"

Paul gripped the boy by the shoulders but found no relief from his swinging feet.

"Brandon!" Elise tried to get to her son.

Paul's voice stopped her. "Elise, let me handle this."

"Brandon," he called out over the child's screams. "Brandon!"

The little boy kept on kicking and screaming, tears running down his cheeks. "It's all your fault."

Just when Elise couldn't take it anymore, Paul lifted Brandon and wrapped him in a hug tight enough the boy couldn't move his arms or legs. He grunted his frustration, the tears coursing. "If you hadn't come, this wouldn't have happened."

"No, Brandon." Elise moved up behind him and laid a hand on his back. "Someone is trying to scare us."

"It's him!"

"No, Paul is here to protect us. Aunt Brenna sent him. He helped us up in North Dakota. He'll help us now."

"No, he's the one doing this."

"No, sweetheart, he's not. Agent Fletcher is one of the good guys."

Brandon looked into Paul's eyes, his own blue eyes filled with distrust. "You took Daddy away, didn't you?"

"Brandon, your dad died in a fire."

"No, he didn't!" Brandon shot an accusing glance at Elise.

The force of the look almost made her stagger. She couldn't deny Brandon's claim. With the notes and the woman who'd disappeared, she truly believed her husband was back and that he wanted revenge.

The anger and hurt dissolved as he stared at her. "Mom, is it true? Did our dad kill all those women?"

Elise's heart broke into a million pieces. She'd never wanted her sons to know the extent of their father's horrible legacy.

"Brandon, some people get sick in ways that aren't like a cold or flu. They get sick here." Paul loosened his grip enough to touch his finger to his temple.

Brandon switched his attention to Paul, the frown still furrowing his young brow. "Like crazy people?"

"Yes." Elise pounced on that. "Your father couldn't help it. His brain was sick."

Brandon pushed against Paul's arms. "You can put me down. I won't hurt you."

If Elise weren't so upset, she would have smiled at the little boy telling the hulking agent he wouldn't hurt him.

Brandon stood there, all straight and serious, like a little old man, not a boy of eight. "Am I going to get sick like my father?"

Elise dropped to her knees and pulled her son into her arms. "No, Brandon. You are not going to get sick like your father."

He pushed her to arm's length. "What about Luke? Is he going to get sick like our father?"

Tears welled in Elise's eyes. "No, baby, you both

are going to be just fine. You'll grow up into wonderful, loving men and have children and families who love you."

Brandon stood for a long moment, staring into his mother's eyes, seeking reassurance. Finally, he nodded. "I'd better go check on Luke."

"That's a good idea." Elise stood, scrubbing the tears from her eyes. "Please have him come inside, will you?"

As Brandon turned toward the back door, Paul laid a hand on his shoulder. "You have a mighty good kick."

Brandon hung his head and scuffed his shoe against the carpet. "I'm sorry, Mr. Fletcher. I shouldn't have done that."

"It's okay. At least I know you can defend your mother like a pro."

Brandon looked up at Paul, his eyes burning fiercely bright. "I won't let anyone hurt her."

"And nor will I. I promise." Paul held out his hand, man-to-man.

With all the dignity of a statesman, Brandon shook Paul's hand. Then he ran for the back door, yelling, "Luke! Luke, you get in here right now!"

Elise faced her bedroom again and pushed the door open. "It's another note."

Paul nodded. "Yeah."

Elise shivered, her thoughts going back to the spring in North Dakota as one woman after another disappeared, only to be found dead days later. "If he follows the same pattern as last time, he's going to kill again," she whispered.

When Paul didn't answer, she looked up into his eyes. "How can we keep him from taking another woman?"

For a moment, Paul refused to meet her gaze. When he did, his blue eyes were the flat color of slate. "We can't."

Elise's heart flipped over, all the blood leaving her head in a rush. She leaned a hand against the wall to steady herself. "Dear God. He already has another."

Paul nodded. "Last night."

CHAPTER 10

"Ms. Johnson, mind if we come in?" Two students Paul had seen in Elise's class appeared at the back door of her house, one on each side of Luke, each holding one of his hands.

"Mom, watch this!" Luke reared back and swung forward, kicking his feet high in the air. He flipped over and landed on his feet, still holding onto the teens' hands.

Paul muttered a curse beneath his breath for the untimely interruption. He'd wanted to reassure Elise in some way before she faced the others.

"Wow, Luke, that's amazing." Elise's voice was strained, not her typical soft, melodious sound and her face had lost most of its color. "Kendall, Alex, what brings you here?"

The young man held up a notebook. "You wouldn't believe all the information Kenny and I have come up with on Jack the Ripper. We are *so* going to make an A on our research paper."

Paul opened the screen door, cringing inwardly at the subject Alex mentioned. Jack the Ripper? Why do a research paper on a killer who was never caught? He glanced at Elise.

Her mouth turned up on the corners, though her lips looked a bit too tight for the smile to be natural.

As he held the door for the kid, Luke shot through and headed straight for his room. "Alex, come see the Spider-Man action figure Aunt Brenna sent me," he yelled over his shoulder.

"I will, in a minute." Alex grinned, following Kendall through the door. "I had a collection of Spider-Man and Hulk action figures when I was a kid. I know, it's hard to picture now." He tipped his head to the side. "Come to think of it, I might still have them buried in my closet. I should dig them out. Luke might like them."

Kendall turned toward the door. "Brandon, aren't you coming in?"

A sullen Brandon tromped up the steps and entered.

Paul released the door and stood back.

"Brandon, go wash your hands for dinner, please," Elise said.

When the boy complied without argument, Paul knew he probably was still traumatized by the writing on the wall in Elise's bedroom. He gave her door a wide berth as he passed, his gaze flickering to the wall inside.

Kendall's pale brows inched up her forehead. "You don't mind, do you? Us coming over and all?"

Elise waved her hand absently, her gaze dull. "No, not at all. But do your parents know where you are?"

"Yeah, I told Mom I was going to get some help on my history homework." Kendall beamed. "Not that I need help on that. I totally get it."

"Uh, good, good." Elise's gaze flickered to Paul.

Paul stepped toward Elise and almost put his arm around her when he had second thoughts in front of the teens. "Maybe now isn't a good time. Ms. Johnson is having an unusually bad day and needs some time to wind down."

Kendall touched Elise's arm. "Is that why your makeup is all smeared? I didn't want to say anything."

Elise scrubbed at her eyes and gave a shaky laugh. "That bad, is it?"

"No, not really, just a little black around the corners. But your eyes are a little red-rimmed, too." Kendall's lips compressed into a line. "Does your bad day have to do with what happened in class?"

Alex stepped closer. "Caesar was out of line. He shouldn't have threatened you."

Paul sent a piercing look at Elise. "What happened in class?"

She shrugged, her lips twisting. "One of my students has anger management issues."

Alex harrumphed. "Understatement of the year, if you ask me."

Every protective instinct in Paul rose with the hairs on the back of his neck. "Was he the kid being chased across campus by the campus cop?"

"You saw that?" Alex's eyes widened.

"Yeah." Paul's gaze remained on Elise. "I spoke with the police officer, too."

Kendall nodded. "That would be our Caesar. Jumped out of the window of the classroom when Officer West came in. Did he catch him?"

"Unfortunately, no." Paul faced Elise. "Could he be the one who threw the brick?"

Elise shrugged. "I told you, I don't know. I didn't see who threw it. Like I said, I was looking in the rearview mirror."

Looking for him. Paul could have kicked himself for not tailing her more closely.

"Brick?" Kendall latched onto the word, her gaze on Elise's pale face. "Someone threw a brick? Did it hit you?"

"No, it didn't hit me. It did hit the windshield of my car," she said, her voice low. She shot a glance toward the hallway where the boys had disappeared.

"I'm glad you're okay, anyway." Kendall wrapped her arms around Elise and hugged her. "That jerk should be kicked out of school."

"Alex, are you gonna come see my Spider-Man?" Luke called out from his bedroom.

Alex grinned. "Guess I better check it out."

Elise gave him a wan smile. "Thanks."

Alex sauntered down the hall, peering into the open bedroom doors. "Where are you, Luke?"

"In here!" Luke shouted.

Before Alex arrived at Luke's door farther down the hallway, he came to a sudden halt in front of Elise's bedroom door.

"Wait, Alex!" Elise lunged toward the teen.

Paul realized their mistake at about the same time as Elise and they collided at the entrance to the hallway.

Alex stood transfixed, staring into the bedroom. "Wow, Ms. Johnson. Someone did a number on your wall."

"It's nothing." Elise reached for the door handle, but before she could close the door, Kendall ducked around her and entered.

"Holy crap!" the blond-haired teen said, her jaw-dropping. "Who did this?"

Elise stared at Paul, her eyes pooling with more tears. "I don't know."

"Oh, my God!" Kendall's hand covered her mouth. "Does this have to do with the woman they found dead? She was a blonde, wasn't she?" Kendall faced Elise, her eyes wide. "Was this why you were all creeped out when I stopped by the other day?"

Paul pulled Elise into the crook of his arm,

unconcerned about what the teens might think of their relationship.

Her body shook as though she were chilled. "Yes."

"Oh, Ms. Johnson." Kendall reached for her hands and held them. "This is terrible. Did you go to the police?"

"She went to the FBI," Paul answered for Elise.

Alex's eyes rounded. "You're an FBI agent?"

Paul nodded.

"Wow." Alex's teeth shone in a huge grin. "That's so cool."

"Alex! Ms. Johnson could be in trouble. She's blond and everything, like the note on the wall."

Alex looked at her sideways. "Kenny, so are you, in case you didn't notice. And so are half the girls at school."

Kenny's face blanched. "That's right." She stood for a moment, staring at the wall, then she reached into her back pocket and pulled out her cell phone and held it up and clicked a button.

"What are you doing?" Elise grabbed her arm and pulled it down.

"Getting a picture." Kendall turned the phone over and viewed the picture she'd just taken. "We could be involved in an honest-to-God murder case. This is evidence."

Elise snatched the cell phone from Kenny's hand. "You can't show this to anyone."

"Why? It's part of solving the case. The police need to see it."

"I have my reasons." Elise clicked the buttons on the phone, trying to delete the picture. "How do you delete it? You have to delete it!"

"It's okay, Ms. Johnson." Kendall reached around and touched her finger to two buttons. The display asked to cancel or delete. Kendall pressed the key for delete and the picture of Elise's wall disappeared. "I'm sorry. I wouldn't have taken the picture if I'd known it would upset you so much."

"No, I'm sorry." Elise shoved the phone back in Kendall's hands. "I shouldn't have overreacted."

"Is there anything we can do? Do you want me to keep the boys while you talk with the police?" Kendall asked. "I've had the Red Cross CPR and babysitting courses."

"No, no. We'll manage." Elise placed a hand on Kendall's arm and one on Alex's. "Please, don't say anything to anyone about this. Please."

"We won't, Ms. Johnson," Alex answered automatically.

Kendall bit on her bottom lip but didn't say anything.

Alex jabbed her in the ribs. "Right, Kenny?"

The teen frowned and rubbed her ribs. "Right, right. We won't tell anyone. But I think you need to take it to the police."

Elise's hand fluttered up to Paul's chest. "I have the FBI working on it. They know what to do."

Paul grabbed her hand and held it trapped against his shirt, wishing he'd thought to close the door before Alex and Kendall saw the writing. The more people knew about it, the more likely it would get around. Elise's new life looked to be blowing wide open.

Alex grabbed Kendall's arm and pulled her toward the door. "Come on, Kendall. Ms. Johnson has enough to worry about. Let's go home."

"Thanks, Alex," Elise said. "I'll see you two tomorrow."

"Seven-thirty, right?" Kendall asked.

Elise's brow furrowed. "Seven-thirty?"

"Didn't you need help setting up for a movie?"

Elise softly snorted, her smile unconvincing. "Yes, yes I did."

"We'll be there," Alex said.

"Good, I might need help with the old audio-visual equipment. We're supposed to watch a DVD I found in the library for class tomorrow and I haven't a clue how to work the machine."

Alex's face lit up. "Cool! I like working with antique electronics." Then he toned down his enthusiasm, his face getting serious. "Be careful, Ms. Johnson."

Elise leaned against Paul and tears glistened in the

corners of her eyes. "Thanks, Alex, Kendall. Go straight home, will you?"

Kendall's shoulders pushed back, and her jaw set firmly. "Don't worry, Ms. Johnson." She dragged Alex out the front door and the room faded into silence.

"I guess I should be packing my bags." Elise pulled away from Paul and stood looking around her living room, her eyes swimming with unshed tears.

Paul reached for her, but she stepped away. "You can't give up now."

"I feel as though there is a line forming to throw more bricks my way."

"I'd say the brick was the act of a juvenile—an angry juvenile."

"You think it was Caesar?" Elise nodded. "Yeah, you're probably right. He likes to scare people. It's the only way he knows how to get attention." Her gaze went to the bathroom, where the door opened and Brandon came out, his hands wet and dripping. Her eyes shone with love for her son. She'd do anything for her boys.

Her oldest son glanced their way. After a long moment, he ducked into the bedroom he shared with Luke.

Elise's shoulders sagged. "What am I going to do?"

"What you always do. Stand tall and make sure your boys are okay." If he could, Paul would wrap her in his arms and shield her from all that was bad in the world, shoulder her burdens so she didn't have to. But she'd pushed him away, determined to manage her fear alone, and he had a job to do. Standing around here wasn't getting it done. "Are you going to be all right until nightfall? I have to go to the office and check on a few things. I'll be back before eleven tonight."

"I'll keep the door locked."

"Good. And don't open it for anyone but me."

"Don't worry," she said in a tone low enough Brandon wouldn't overhear. "I'm scared enough now to follow orders."

"And I know this won't make you feel any better but leave the note on the wall. I want someone from our forensics team to take a look at it."

Elise shook her head. "No."

"Okay, how about I get Mel to catalog the evidence, take pictures and run it through evidence with the location undisclosed. Deal?"

Elise chewed on her lower lip, the action making him want to taste that lip himself. "Okay. But just Mel."

"I'll have her here as soon as possible." He turned for the door.

"Paul?" her voice pulled him back to stand in front of her.

"Yes?"

She stared up at him through dew-kissed blue eyes. "Thanks." She leaned up on her toes and pressed a sweet kiss to his lips.

Paul fought the urge to crush her in his arms and deepen the kiss. Instead, he ended the kiss and stepped away. "You don't have to thank me. It's my job."

Elise's tears trickled out of the corners of her eyes, then turned and fled for the boys' bedroom.

As Paul closed the front door behind him, Luke's voice called out, muffled by the heavy wood door, "Hey, where'd Alex go? I wanted to show him my Spider-Man."

A smile crossed Paul's face. A boy like Luke would be fine no matter what. Brandon knew too much for his own good. That child acted more like an old man.

Anger surged in Paul's gut. The boy's childhood had been stolen from him by his abusive father and now by this new threat.

And Elise...how much torture could one woman stand? The fear she must be feeling had to be overwhelming.

Paul climbed into his truck and headed for the sheriff's office. He had to tell Sheriff Engel about the notes. Holding back information was almost as bad as committing the crime.

* * *

ELISE WANDERED AROUND THE HOUSE, checking each window lock, door lock and deadbolt. Her cozy little house felt more like a cage than a home. She needed a fortress, not a house of sticks.

The cell phone rang. She hurried to answer, thinking it might be Paul with another round of cautions. She didn't care, she felt more secure in his presence, even when it was only his voice. The caller ID displayed "Unknown".

"Did you forget something?" she asked, her voice slightly breathless, the feel of Paul's lips still tingling on hers.

"No, I remember every detail." The voice wasn't Paul's. It was mechanical and disguised. "Did you like my artwork?"

Cold chills shook Elise so hard her teeth rattled. "Who is this?"

"You know who."

"No, I don't."

"After eight years of marital bliss, you'd forget me so soon?"

"My husband is dead."

"Are you sure I'm dead? Did you bury me yourself? Did you see my body?"

"No," she whispered, her hand shaking so hard she almost dropped the telephone.

"Does the fed make you scream in bed like I did?"

"Shut up! My husband is dead."

"Does he make you cry out his name?" the mechanical voice said.

"None of your business!"

"Get rid of the new boyfriend, Alice. He'll never be enough man for you. He didn't catch me. He's not the hero everyone makes him out to be."

"What do you know about being a man? Do you think real men are supposed to hurt women?" She forced a laugh she didn't feel. "Any man who hurts women is a coward. You must be afraid of other men, if you have to hurt women to get off."

She must have struck a chord in him because the phone remained silent for several long moments.

"Do you hear me?" Elise turned away from her boys' bedroom door and walked into the kitchen, placing distance between her children and her. They didn't need to know. They shouldn't have to know. "You're a coward."

"Don't make me mad, Alice."

"Why? Can't you take it like a man?" Why didn't she just shut up? Why was she egging on a killer? Why was she so angry? Because her anger masked her fear, stiffened her spine and made her want to take action.

Elise Johnson was tired of being afraid. Tired of running. Tired of men controlling her life. "Leave me the hell alone."

"Sorry, baby. I can't." The mechanical voice breathed into the phone, the static crackling in Elise's ear. "Say goodbye to pretty Mary Alice."

A woman screamed in the background.

"No! Wait!" Elise gulped past the horror clogging her throat.

"Change your mind? Want me to visit you instead?"

"No! Don't hurt that woman. Please."

"Why? Are you willing to take her place?"

Elise thought of her boys. If she gave herself to this maniac, they'd be orphaned. "Don't hurt her. It's me you want, not her."

"True, but I want you to suffer like you made me suffer."

"What do you want from me? Why are you doing this?"

"Like the rhyme said..." He laughed. "They remind me of everything I lost because of you...Alice."

CHAPTER 11

Paul strode through the office, heels hitting hard on the tiled floor. "Mel? You here?"

Mel's head popped up over the top of her cubicle. "I'm here, though I'd rather be out of this stuffy office. Whatcha got?"

"In my office, ASAP." He paced behind his desk until Mel closed the door.

She stood with her shoulders back, her hands crossed at the small of her back in a perfect parade rest. "What happened, boss?"

"Whoever left Elise that note, broke into her home and wrote another across the wall in her bedroom."

"Shoot." Mel let out a long breath. "The woman could use some better locks."

"I need you out there as soon as possible to collect

any evidence you can find. And get a locksmith. I want all the doors on her house rekeyed."

"I should get hold of Joe in Forensics."

"No, I promised her we wouldn't get more people involved than we already have. She's expecting you and the sooner you're out there, the better I'll feel."

"Gotcha." Mel dug a small steno pad out of her back jeans pocket. "I spent my day out in Breuer as well, interviewing the first victim's friends and family. It seems Lauren Alice Pendley worked in the high school cafeteria as a lunch lady. She quit just a month ago to go to work at the pharmacy."

"Elise's high school?"

Mel nodded. "One and the same."

"I think I need to spend more time on campus."

"On campus in general, or with Elise in particular?" Mel's smile came and went with the searing glare Paul aimed her way. "Anything else, boss?"

"Yeah, keep an eye open for a Hispanic teen about six feet tall. Caesar Valdez. He threatened Elise in school today and I think he was also responsible for throwing a brick at her car windshield."

"Think our Alice Klaus has enough people gunning for her?" Mel shook her head. "And here I thought you were just out enjoying the cool hill-country weather."

Paul ran a hand through his hair, his shoulders tense, the muscles screaming for the release of a good workout. And maybe a workout would help him clear his mind and body of the feeling of Elise's lips on his, her body pressed to him. He really needed to clear his mind of her. If he hurried through the paperwork, he might get in a run before dark. "She's scared, Mel. Go easy on her."

"You don't have to tell me, Paul. I can just imagine. Seems like the world is gangin' up on her."

"Tread lightly around the kids, too. The oldest boy knows about his father."

Mel sucked air past her clamped teeth. "That's a darn shame. Gotta be a blow to the kid to know that much."

"Yeah." Paul frowned at Mel. "When did you start talking like a Texan?"

Mel shrugged. "It grows on you."

He glared at her. "Quit it, it doesn't sound right on someone from the east coast."

"You might not like Texas, but I plan on staying here as long as the Bureau lets me." She hooked her thumbs in the belt loops of her jeans and rocked back on her cowboy boot heels.

Paul shook his head. "Go on. I don't like Elise being without protection too long."

"You kinda like her, don't you?"

Paul jerked his thumb toward the door. "Get the hell out of here, will ya?" As soon as Mel closed the door behind her, Paul stared down at his desk.

A neat stack of papers sat in the middle with a

note on top from Agent Cain. *Assignment complete. Next?*

He rose to check Trevor's desk. The man wasn't there, the desk was clean and the pencils neatly standing in a coffee mug. What did he expect that every agent in the office should work overtime every night like him?

"He's been gone most of the day." Alvarez walked up behind Paul.

"Working the fraud case?" Paul held out his hand to Agent Alvarez.

Alvarez shook his hand and nodded toward Cain's empty desk. "That's what I thought, but I called one of the witnesses he was supposed to talk to today and he hadn't seen him. I called some of the others Cain was supposed to have checked with and they all said the same thing. Did you give him an alternate mission?"

"No." He'd have to talk with Cain first thing in the morning. Paul sighed. He really needed to spend more time with the man and either mentor or transfer him. Cain obviously had an issue with his new boss and assignments.

The cell phone clipped to his belt buzzed. "Fletcher."

"We found Mary Alice." Sheriff Engel's voice came across the line old and tired.

Paul scrubbed a hand over his face, his chest

constricting, making it hard for him to breathe. "Where?"

"Same river, different bridge. And the body's fresh." The sheriff called out orders, his voice muffled by a hand over the receiver. "He's getting sloppy."

"How's that?"

"It's not dark yet and we have a witness who may have seen the vehicle drive away."

"Yeah? Did they get a make and model?"

"Not a make and model, but he said a dark SUV, either black or navy blue, entered the highway from the access road beside the river bridge around five-thirty this afternoon."

"Did they get a license plate?"

"No." The sheriff paused. "Does the FBI have anything they want to share about this case? What about the idea you suggested about this being a copycat of the Dakota Strangler? Anything new in that department?"

"As a matter of fact, I was just about to call you. I need a favor."

After the sheriff agreed to keep Elise's identity secret, Paul filled him in on the notes and the writing on the wall.

"Agent Fletcher, you know I'll have to see it," Sheriff Engel said.

"I know. I have Agent Bradley on her way out to collect the evidence. I'll have her let you in."

"If it helps, I'll swing by my house, change into plain clothes and then head over to Ms. Johnson's."

"Thanks, Sheriff." Paul agreed to meet with him the following day to compare notes and clues. In the meantime, he had duties as the head of the regional office to complete before he returned to Breuer.

He hung up and called his buddy, Agent Nick Tarver.

"I was about to call you." Nick didn't bother with pleasantries. It wasn't his style.

Paul grinned. "Good to hear from you, too."

"I didn't find anything. No John Does, Smiths or Jones checked into any hospitals downstream of the flooding with burn wounds or smoke inhalation during the six weeks following the flood two years ago."

"What about the hospitals within a 200-mile radius?"

"Checked them. No one fitting his description. No unidentified patients, no one in a coma with burns or smoke inhalation there either."

"Nobody, no patient lying in a hospital. Nothing," Paul voiced his thoughts aloud.

"You got it."

"This guy has to be a copycat."

"Agreed. Brenna checked out the local library of all the books written that mention the Dakota Strangler. Each of them details how the victim was strangled and tied up with an Ethernet cable."

"Yeah, but the Dakota Strangler strangled his victims *with* the cable, then tied them with the murder weapon."

"This guy didn't?"

"The first victim was strangled, the coroner thinks with an arm around her throat. No signs of the cable around her throat. Then she was bound at the hands and feet and tossed into the Guadalupe River."

Nick heaved a sigh. "Not quite the same."

"Which could mean something or nothing. It's been two years. If Stan Klaus is still alive, he might have changed his method. Then again, if it's a copycat, how did he find out Elise Johnson is really Alice Klaus?" Paul paused to breathe. "Hell, I didn't even know who she was and where she'd relocated until you and Brenna called."

"Any chance the kids inadvertently let it slip?"

Paul hesitated. Brandon knew his father had killed. "Maybe. But to whom? They go to elementary school. So far, the victims have all had some connection to the high school in some way."

"How big is Breuer?"

"Just under ten thousand people."

"A small town where everyone knows everyone else's business?"

"Not quite. Most of the people who live here in the hill country commute to San Antonio. It's like a really large suburb of the city."

"Still, word could have gotten around."

Paul didn't like the idea of questioning Brandon, but he had to follow all the leads. "I'll see what I can find out."

He ended the call and had just set his cell phone down when it rang again. The name on the caller ID made him pick up. "What's wrong, Elise?"

"I got a call from him."

The tone of Elise's voice told Paul all he needed to know about who "him" was.

Paul gripped the phone hard. "Tell me."

* * *

ELISE BUSIED herself with getting the boys through homework and their nightly routine. She didn't want to slow down long enough to think about what the killer had said, nor did she want to relive the scream she'd heard in the background. She'd probably hear that scream echoing in her nightmares for the rest of her life.

Promptly at eight-thirty, she had Luke and Brandon bathed and tucked into their beds, forcing herself to take the time to read a story to them, when all she wanted was to run screaming through the house. Normalcy was what they needed in their lives. Normalcy was what she prayed for every day, though her prayers had gone unanswered.

Agent Melissa Bradley had called thirty minutes earlier to say she'd be there around eight forty-five with the sheriff.

The entire time Elise read to her boys, her thoughts strayed to that phone call and anger surged through her veins. Surged and ebbed away and surged again.

She knew she had to tell the police about the notes and the phone call, but still Elise couldn't help dreading the exposure of her and her children to the scrutiny of the police and, ultimately the press.

Elise leaned over Brandon and kissed his forehead. Nowadays, he only let her kiss him when he was sleeping. Kissing was for babies, and Brandon was the man of the house. She'd told him so and he'd taken his responsibilities seriously.

Elise stared down at him as he lay snuggled in his twin-sized bed, the exact match of his brother's beside him. Her heart swelled with the pain and love she felt for her sons.

Brandon knew. All this time, she'd avoided talking with Brandon about what had happened back in North Dakota. She'd hoped he'd forgotten, that his young mind would let it go. Maybe he wouldn't remember the news reporters pushing microphones into his mother's face, asking her if she'd known that her husband had been killing women.

He'd probably seen the reports on television

displaying the picture of his father, calling him the Dakota Strangler. What must that have done to him? And for Brandon to hold that inside all this time must have been hard.

A lump choked her throat. She struggled to swallow past it.

She'd thought moving this far south, where no one knew her and her sons, would safeguard them from the torment of the press. Never in a million years had she imagined that her husband might still be alive and want revenge on her for hiding his sons.

Elise scrubbed at the tears now streaming down her cheeks.

Would this nightmare ever end?

She trudged into the living room and stared around at the scattered toys, shoes and books, with no desire to clean. The familiar creaking sound the house made occasionally made her jump. A cat squalled outside the window, sending shivers up and down Elise's arms. Despite her desire for independence, she found herself clock-watching, waiting for Paul's return. In the meantime, she couldn't sit around twitching at every noise.

Elise switched on the television to mask the noises of the encroaching night. No sooner had she tuned into a favorite sitcom and settled into her lounge chair, than she got a shock during the first commercial break.

A San Antonio anchorman looked into the camera, but Elise felt as if he were talking directly to her. "Another young woman was found murdered in the Guadalupe River this afternoon. Stay tuned to the news at ten for more on this breaking story."

Elise's heart fisted in her gut, churning the mac and cheese she'd eaten for dinner into bile. The sick bastard had killed Mary Alice. She doubled over and moaned. No. This couldn't be happening.

A soft knock sounded from the front door, jerking her out of her anguish and back into stark terror.

Her heart hammering in her chest, Elise leaped to her feet and ran for the door. Her hand paused on the knob. She didn't have a peephole to identify the person on the other side. "Who is it?" she said, inwardly cursing how much her voice shook.

"Elise, it's me, Melissa Bradley."

Elise crossed to the window and parted the vinyl blinds.

Agent Bradley stood in her faded blue jeans, crisp white blouse, navy-blue wool blazer and mock-ostrich-skin cowboy boots. Behind her stood an older man in sweatpants and a sweatshirt with Kendall Country Sheriff written in bold black letters over his right breast.

Darkness crept in on the quiet street, edging out the last rays of sun. Wind buffeted the gnarled live oak in the front yard. For all her neighbors knew, two normal people had shown up to pay Elise Johnson a visit. Not that it mattered. Elise couldn't keep her identity a secret much longer. Not when the lives of more women were at stake.

She sighed and unlocked the deadbolt, relieved and apprehensive at the same time. "Please, come in."

Melissa entered with a camera around her neck, carrying what looked like a toolbox. She turned to the man behind her. "Elise Johnson, this is Kendall County Sheriff Thomas Engel."

The sheriff held out a meaty hand and nodded. "Ms. Johnson. I understand you've had some trouble. I'm here to help."

Elise shook hands with the sheriff dreading the questioning to come, yet knowing it had to be addressed. "If you'll follow me. Please try to keep it down, the boys are sleeping."

"We'll make this as painless as possible. Unfortunately, some of this stuff can be messy." Agent Bradley nodded. "Lead the way."

When Elise opened the door to her bedroom, a cold wave of dread swept her all over again. The lettering hadn't changed since Brandon found it earlier that day, yet it hung over her bed, taunting her with an oppressive threat.

Melissa set the toolbox on the floor, then started snapping pictures. "Has anything been disturbed since you found it?"

"No." She hadn't even gone into her room since Alex and Kendall had been there.

"Good." Melissa covered the room's every angle and closed in on the writing on the wall.

Elise tried to imagine what the room looked like from Mel's viewpoint. A full-sized bed in the middle of the room. Only one pillow, fluffy yellow bedding and a child's action figure lying on the nightstand. Lonely, female, single parent without a sex life.

On her limited budget, Elise had gone for soft and feminine decor. The exact opposite of what Stan had insisted she buy for their bedroom. She hadn't wanted to be reminded of her former husband in any way whatsoever, preferring to completely erase him from her existence. So much for erasing him. "Sheriff, the news said another woman was found this afternoon."

"Good news travels fast." The lines around his eyes deepened. "Bad news even faster."

"Was she a blonde, Sheriff Engel?" Elise asked, her voice barely above a whisper, as her gaze traveled over the writing on the wall and her mind rolled over the words the killer had spoken on the phone only a few short hours ago.

The sheriff stared at the message on the wall and nodded, his lips set in a grim line. "Yes, ma'am."

"And the woman from the other day?" Elise knew the answer before she asked.

"Blondes on both counts." The sheriff flipped

open a notepad and jotted something down. "Seems we might have us a serial killer with a penchant for blondes on our hands."

Blondes by the name of Alice.

Elise stood outside her bedroom, not sure she'd ever be able to sleep there again. "Whoever killed those two women was in this house."

Melissa dropped to her haunches beside the toolbox and flipped the metal latches open. "I have a locksmith on his way. Should be here any minute. The boss wants to make sure you're rekeyed and secure before you go to bed tonight, or we could move you and the boys to a safe house."

A small amount of relief loosened some of the tension in her shoulders. "No thanks. New locks will be sufficient." At least she could rest somewhat assured the killer wouldn't have a key to the new locks.

Elise paced the hallway, stopping to peek in on the boys who slept oblivious to the visitors. Thank goodness. How would she convince Brandon that everything was all right when their world was falling apart around them?

When she returned, Melissa was brushing black powder on surfaces throughout the room. "I'm sorry, this is a mess, but I'm hoping we'll find a fingerprint or two."

"I don't mind. I'd like to know how he got in," Elise stated.

"We would, too." Melissa dusted black powder on the wall near the writing. "Did you check all your windows and doors before you left this morning?"

"Ever since I got the first note, I've been very careful to lock everything."

"Are you certain the kids didn't unlock a window or leave a door unlocked?"

"I double-checked everything before we left for school."

Melissa shook her head. "Then he's either good at lock-picking or he's got a master key similar to what a locksmith would carry."

"Are you telling me new locks won't keep him out?" Elise laughed, although no amount of humor reflected in the sound. "That's reassuring."

"I'd get the new locks, just in case he's gotten hold of one of your keys from somewhere."

"Where?"

"Do you leave your keys with a garage attendant when you get your oil changed?" the sheriff asked.

"No, I only leave my car key."

Sheriff Engel made a note on his pad. "Do you keep a spare house key anywhere?"

"Only at school in my desk drawer and I keep that locked when I'm not there."

"Have you checked that lock lately to be sure someone hasn't tampered with it?"

"No, it never occurred to me."

"I wouldn't put it past this guy." Melissa shrugged.

"I wouldn't put anything past this guy. You might consider buying a big dog or a gun."

"I'm seriously considering a gun." Then she told Mel and the sheriff about her phone conversation with the killer.

CHAPTER 12

PAUL PARKED along the side of the street a block over from Elise's house. He wanted to get a quick run in before he called it a night and camped out on her couch.

He climbed out of his truck, wearing a pair of gray shorts and a plain gray T-shirt. The wind whipped across his biceps, raising goose bumps along his exposed skin. He debated the sweatshirt on the backseat but decided against it. Fifty-five degrees didn't bother him as long as he kept moving. After the months of record heat, a little cold air would be refreshing. And he needed to move to get rid of the cobwebs crowding his thoughts so that he could think more clearly and get some perspective on this case.

He took off at a steady jog. Darkness claimed the day, settling like a shroud over the small town. He'd told Melissa he'd work out before he arrived at Elise's house and that Elise should expect him around ten o'clock. Instead of jogging the track close to his apartment in San Antonio, he'd decided to take his workout to Breuer and make some use of it, scouting the neighborhood around the Johnson's house.

Melissa had informed him that she'd completed collecting evidence and the sheriff had asked all the questions he could possibly ask Elise. The locksmith had come and gone, leaving brand new locks on all the doors and giving his nod over the ones on the windows. All that and the boys hadn't woken up once.

Paul smiled, not surprised that Luke hadn't woken up, knowing how busy the little guy was when he was awake. The kid could sleep through a tornado, with as much energy as he burned during the day.

Brandon, on the other hand, was an entirely different case. Paul would have thought any little sound would wake the older of the two boys. Given the amount of emotional trauma he'd experienced finding the note on the wall and owning up to the knowledge of his father's career as a killer, the kid probably had nightmares.

Only a block over from Elise's little cottage, Paul found himself headed her way first. As soon as he turned west, the wind thrust against him, penetrating the single layer of his T-shirt and chilling his skin. He picked up the pace, passing the front of her house, pushing hard to encourage his body to warm quickly.

From the outside, all was peaceful, inside a frightened woman was probably pacing the floor, wondering where the killer would strike next.

He lengthened his stride, passing half a dozen little houses. At the next street, he turned left and made another left on the street running parallel to Highland.

He wanted to see the house behind hers. With all the brush and overgrown hedges, he'd only glimpsed the rooftop. If the house was anything like the hedges, it would probably be run down and in need of work.

The opposite was the case. The house behind Elise's was a single-story dwelling spread out over the lot. The yard and garden in front were well-maintained and neatly kept. Whoever took care of the front yard obviously didn't have a hand in the care of the backyard. Two rockers sat on the front porch, rocking gently in the wind.

Paul slowed to a stop beneath the heavy limbs of a bare native pecan tree and stared into the shadowy backyard.

Luke had stood at his back fence, calling through the hedges to someone on this side. But who? Paul made a note to introduce himself to this neighbor.

As he studied the house, he didn't get any idea

about its occupants from its neat appearance. If anything, he'd guess a little old lady lived there who liked to sit on the porch and rock during the warmer weather. But then, who was the guy Luke referred to as George? A little boy?

Paul saw no signs of a little boy. No toys or swing set in the yard, no bicycle propped against the house. He moved toward the backyard, careful to be quiet and not disturb the occupants. He didn't need to scare an old woman into a heart attack, thinking she had a peeping tom. As he peered into the darkness of the backyard, ancient live oaks and native pecan trees cast impenetrable, inky shadows.

Paul squinted, his eyes struggling to adjust to the limited light of the dark yard beyond. Hunkering low and keeping away from the few beams of light cast across the grass by the streetlight out front, he moved toward the side of the house, blending with the bushes lining the boundary.

Movement caught the corner of his eye. It wasn't in the backyard of this house but in Elise's.

Adrenaline spiked in Paul's veins, shooting through his muscles, warming them from the inside out. He ran for the back row of overgrown bushes and hedges. The more he pushed and shoved, the more he realized he wasn't getting through them and had to go around.

Angry at having wasted even a minute trying to push through, Paul sprinted back around the line of bushes to close on Elise's house. The shadow had disappeared by the time he got there.

A vehicle engine revved in the distance. Paul raced out to the pavement in time to see brake lights flash before they disappeared around a dark corner. The driver hadn't bothered to turn on the car's exterior lights, no headlights or taillights. What fool would drive around in the dark without their lights on? Someone bent on stirring up trouble. Someone who didn't want to get caught.

Paul ran full out, arriving at the corner in time to see...nothing.

The vehicle had completely vanished.

Breathing hard from the sprint and the anger surging through his body, Paul gave up on his run and hurried back to his truck. If nothing else, having the truck in Elise's driveway should ward off unwanted visits.

Paul pulled up in the driveway and shut off the engine. No sooner had he climbed down from the cab than the blinds flickered in the window.

Before he rounded the truck, the front door opened. Elise stood in the hazy glow of the front porch light, her hair whipped by the wind and shining a golden blur around her head. Her tired smile made his heart flip over and then ram against his chest.

Paul hurried toward her, wanting to pull her into his arms and hold her there until all the bad things stopped. Elise started to take a step, stopped and stared down at something on the front stoop.

Her eyes widened and she froze.

Halfway to her, Paul wondered what she was staring at. His heartbeat kicked up a notch and he rushed forward. "Elise?"

She looked up at him, her eyes filling with tears. "Who is doing this to me?"

On the ground at her feet was a fashion doll with golden blond hair like Elise's, wearing a blue skirt and white blouse like she'd worn earlier that day. What sent cold chills down Paul's spine was the Ethernet cable tied around the doll's neck.

He opened his arms, and she fell into them, sobbing against his chest. Leaving the doll on the stoop, Paul lifted Elise into his arms and carried her across the threshold into the house, kicking the door shut behind him. He set her on her feet and turned to twist the shiny new deadbolt lock, one arm still around her waist, holding her against him.

Elise pressed her face into his T-shirt, her fingers bunching the material in her grip. "Why?" she sobbed quietly.

"I don't know. But it doesn't matter. You are not going to be next on any killer's list."

"I can't die." She laid her cheek against his chest, sniffing loudly. "What would Brandon and Luke do? They only have one parent."

The warmth of her tears soaking his shirt made

him want to shield her from the terror of the day. "You're not going anywhere. You're going to see Brandon and Luke grow up. You'll have the pleasure of suffering when they go through puberty. You'll sprout a few gray hairs, teaching them to drive." Paul stroked the back of her hair, wishing he could be there when she got those gray hairs. He bet she'd be just as beautiful as she was today.

She chuckled. "Oh, please, you're not helping."

He tipped her head up and stared down into her eyes. "You're a good mother, Elise, and I promise I'll do everything in my power to make sure you have the opportunity to raise those boys yourself."

Her blue eyes filled with a fresh wave of tears. "I can't even sleep in my own bedroom. That monster was in there, writing on my wall."

"Then sleep out here." He nodded toward the couch. "You can have the couch. I'll sleep in the lounge chair. Either way, I'm not going anywhere."

She sucked in a long, shaky breath and let it out, resting her forehead against his chest. "I promised myself I wouldn't let another man control my life."

"Is that what you think this is? Me controlling your life?"

"No." She smiled up at him, her eyes awash in unshed tears. "You aren't controlling my life. The killer is. He's making me afraid to step outside my door. Afraid to go to work. Afraid to answer my own telephone."

"We'll get him."

"When? After another woman dies?" Her voice caught in her throat. She glanced toward the hallway where her boys slept. "Or after I die?"

Paul pushed a long strand of golden blond hair behind her ear and bent to press a kiss to her temple. "You're not going to die."

She turned her face to his, their lips only a breath away. "Why do you care? You don't even know me."

With his mouth hovering over hers, he stared into her eyes. "I've known you since I first met you and the boys in North Dakota."

"You were only around for a week, tops."

"It was enough." Since then, she'd haunted his dreams. This beauty had no idea how her sad eyes had penetrated his reserve where women were concerned. Her bravery in the face of the media circus, the accusations, the police hounding her for answers. She'd kept a stiff upper lip, protecting her boys like a mama bear, always composed under the glare of the cameras. She was the kind of woman he'd only dreamed about, the kind a man married and lived with happily ever after. The kind he'd shied away from, certain he had nothing to offer.

But the timing had been way off. Seemed like Paul's timing continued to be off. Yet he couldn't ignore the way she felt, her body pressed against his, her breath warm against his lips.

"I want to..." Her voice trailed off, her eyelids drifting to half-mast. "But I shouldn't."

"No, we shouldn't." He stared into eyes so blue they rivaled the summer sky, his heart pounding against his ribs, the erratic beats having nothing to do with his earlier run. He couldn't control himself. He pulled her against him and kissed her.

At first stiff, Elise pressed her hands to his chest. Then she melted into his arms, her soft moan warming the inside of his mouth, touching him in places he didn't think accessible.

His tongue slipped across the seam of her lips. When they parted, he dove in past the slick smoothness of minty fresh teeth to the warm, soft wetness of her tongue.

Her hands crept up his chest to wrap around his neck, dragging him to her.

He complied, his fingers gripping her hips, pulling her closer. The hard ridge of his erection pressed through the thin material of his shorts, nudging against her belly. Holding her hard against him, one hand crept up beneath her T-shirt, his thumb connecting with the soft swell of her naked breast.

Elise leaned into his touch, her lungs filling, pushing her breasts against his palm.

His thumb found the beaded nipple, and flicked over the tip until Elise gasped into his mouth.

The featherlight touch of her hands slipped down

his back. She grasped the hem of his T-shirt and tugged it upward.

Paul released his hold on her breast and lifted his arms.

Elise tugged the shirt higher.

Impatient to get his hands back on her beautiful body, Paul grabbed the shirt and yanked it over his head, tossing it to the floor.

Elise's eyes widened, her mouth opening on a soft gasp.

For a moment, Paul thought she'd change her mind. He held back, unwilling to push her into anything she might regret. The choice was clearly hers. If she wanted to call a halt at this point...

He sucked in a deep breath and let it out slowly. *So be it.*

Her tongue swept across his lips as she reached out, her fingers weaving into the hairs on his chest. "I want this," she whispered almost too softly to hear.

Paul heard and his body rejoiced. Still, he had to take it slowly, carefully. It took every ounce of his own self-control to keep from ripping clothes off her and making passionate, noisy love to her there on the living room floor.

Her gaze roamed over his chest, her fingers tracing a path to his hard brown nipples. A quick glance over her shoulder must have reassured her that the boys still slept. The door to their bedroom remained firmly closed. "This is so wrong."

He captured her hand beneath his, pressing it against the pounding of his heart. "Then don't." It cost him to make the offer.

"But I want to." She tugged her hand from his and reached for the hem of her shirt, dragging it up her torso.

Every inch the shirt moved exposed pale, silky skin and the curve of her waist. Then a breast appeared and the other. When she raised her arms above her head, Paul could hold back no longer.

With her hands high, the shirt still tangled around her forearms, Paul reached out and cupped both breasts in his palms, a groan rising in his throat. "You're beautiful, Elise."

She tugged the shirt from her arms and let it drop to the floor. "I'm scared."

He kissed the tip of her nose, massaging the rounded flesh weighing lightly in his hands. "Of the killer?" He kissed her, his mouth slanting over hers, his tongue flicking across her lips. "Or me?"

"The killer, yes." Her head dropped back, her hair cascading around her, reaching past her bottom. "But most of all, afraid of myself."

"I won't hurt you," Paul promised. Despite the passion of the moment, threatening to carry him away, he knew how important it was to reassure Elise. "I will never force you to do anything you don't want to."

"That's just it. I want this so much, I can't think."

Her hands ran across his chest in a frenzy, then dipped lower, following the narrowing line of hair to the waistband of his shorts.

Oh, sweet heaven. Paul captured her hand before she went lower. "Don't go there unless you're certain. I can only take so much."

"Paul, I'm not as fragile as you might think." Her shoulders pushed back, forcing her bare breast deeper into his hand. She looked up into his eyes, her own darker than the usual sunny-sky blue, smoldering a smoky gray. "I want this." Her hand skimmed over the hard ridge, making his shorts jut out in a tent. "You obviously want it, so shut up and let me before one of the boys decides to wake up."

Paul grinned and grabbed her around the waist, swinging her around the room, before gently setting her on her feet. "You're an amazing woman."

Elise was feeling pretty amazing, and scared, and filled with an overpowering desire to make love to this man. Now. Before she came to her senses and chickened out. Once he set her back on her feet, she gulped in a fortifying breath and reached for the button on her jeans.

"Let me." His fingers closed over hers and together they flicked it loose, sliding the zipper down to expose the pink lace of her panties.

Elise thanked the laundry gods for the loads of laundry she had yet to wade through. If not for getting behind, she wouldn't have been forced to wear the lacy panties her sister had given her last Christmas instead of the sensible briefs she usually wore.

The jeans came off and she stood in nothing but those stupid pink panties, the cool air raising gooseflesh on her skin.

Paul hooked his thumbs in the elastic waistband of his shorts.

Elise reached out, her fingers colliding with his, sending an electric current all the way up her arms.

He halted the downward progress of his shorts, the elastic catching on that part of him straining for release. "Change your mind?"

Elise shook her head and shoved his hands out of the way. "No. Let me."

She tugged on the front of the shorts, pushing them far enough down his hips that he sprang free.

Her breath caught in her throat. The man was hard, erect and magnificent. Elise hadn't been with any other man but her late husband. But in comparison between the two of them, Paul's muscular body, trim waist and everything else was so much more manly, and larger than life than Stan had ever been.

She curved her hands around his buttocks, sliding the shorts and his briefs over the curve of his muscles and down the backs of his legs. Dropping to her knees, she skimmed over the crisp hairs of his thighs and downward to his taut, well-defined calves.

Paul cupped the back of her head, his fingers

digging into her hair. "I never knew shorts could be so sexy."

"Me, either." She smiled up at him from her position at his feet. Her fingers circled his ankles, pushing the shorts down as he stepped free.

As she rose slowly to her feet, she cupped him in her palm, loving the smooth feel of velvety skin over steely hardness. The juncture between her thighs ached to have him inside her, filling her, making her whole.

"Wait." He leaned over and pulled his wallet from the back pocket of his shorts, slipping a foil packet from its interior.

Elise smiled. "I'm glad you remembered." She had been well on her way to forgetting everything in the moment. That scared her. Was she doing the right thing? Would she be giving Paul the wrong message? Would he expect more from her than she was able to give? More than the sex she so craved? The feel of his body against her, making her remember she was alive and a woman with needs he could satisfy, if only temporarily.

Paul tipped her chin upward and pressed a kiss to her temple. "You're thinking too much." He held her face between his palms, his thumbs stroking her chin, her lips. "Just say no and I'll walk away, no questions asked. I won't be angry."

She stared into his eyes and knew he spoke the truth and knew deep down she was tired of being alone. Tired of being scared and way past due for sex. She inhaled and let the breath out slowly and raised her leg, sliding it along the outside of Paul's calf. Her hands slid over the muscular bulges of his shoulders and upward to wrap around his neck. She laced her fingers behind his head and pulled his mouth down to hers. "Although I appreciate the out you're offering, I think you're talking too much. Shut up and kiss me."

She wrapped her calf around his, rubbing the damp space between her legs over the rough hairs on his thigh. Fire ignited, flaming throughout her body.

Paul's hands slid down her naked backside. He cupped her bottom and lifted her, draping her legs around his waist, his member pressing against her opening. Then he strode across the room, ripped a throw blanket off the back of the couch, tossed it to the carpeted floor and lowered her onto her back.

Elise's feet dropped to the floor.

Paul tore open the packet, removed the condom and rolled it over his engorged staff. He settled between her legs and slid into her, filling her as she'd wanted since he'd entered her home tonight.

He moved in and out of her, gently easing his way deeper and deeper, the speed of his penetration increased until they rocked back and forth in unison.

Tension knotted deep inside her, a sweet, good kind of tension she had never experienced, even with her husband. The knot of pressure built to a ragged edge and then exploded throughout her system, sending shards of pulsing sensations rocketing through her body.

Elise's fingers dug into Paul's shoulders as she rode the wave of feeling until she collapsed against the blanket, gasping for breath. She'd never felt quite this replete. Ever.

As she lay curled in Paul's arms, fear crept back in. Fear for her boys' lives, fear for her own and most of all, perhaps the most frightening of all, fear that she was falling in love. How could she let that happen?

A panic attack big enough to launch a rocket hit her full force. Her chest tightened, her muscles bunched, and she sucked in a deep breath, ready to bolt.

Paul sighed, pulled her close and kissed her on the tip of her nose. "You're going to run, aren't you?" He stared down into her eyes.

She couldn't move, couldn't breathe, couldn't answer his question.

He nodded in answer to his own question and a slow, sad smile crossed his face. "Just know this—I'll let you go now, but I don't give up easily." Paul rolled to his feet and grabbed his shorts, shoving his legs into them.

Elise grabbed her jeans and shirt and ran for the bathroom. She couldn't go back into the living room and face Paul. Not when she didn't know what she wanted from him, from herself, from anything. She couldn't sleep in her bedroom under the writing on the wall aimed to scare her. It had done its job and scared the fool out of her.

Elise washed her face and combed her fingers through her hair, then stepped back out into the living room, dreading facing Paul, completely at a loss for an explanation for her actions.

Paul lay on the couch, his back to her, wrapped in the throw blanket. He didn't budge or acknowledge her presence. And was that him snoring? Elise suspected he was faking to put her at ease.

A smile curled the corners of her mouth. Grabbing a blanket from the hall closet, Elise slipped into the lounge chair and lay back. Her body still hummed from making love with Paul and danged if she didn't want to do it again. But she couldn't. Not now.

Not when she suspected she was falling in love with him.

CHAPTER 13

ALEX DUMPED his backpack on the floor beside the roller cart with the television on it. "Ms. Johnson, where's the DVD you wanted to play for the class?"

"I left it in the machine yesterday afternoon. I couldn't figure out how to make the video display on the screen. Think you can work some magic on it?"

Elise had arrived on time, but everything conspired against her getting the audio-visual equipment going for her first class. Thank goodness her first class was actually the second hour of the day and not the first. Alex and Kendall served as her assistants during their study hall.

Elise knew teachers weren't supposed to show favoritism to students, however, Alex and Kendall were always willing to help and loved learning. How could she not favor them? And they helped keep her mind off the writing on her wall and what she'd done with Paul on the floor of her living room last night.

Her cheeks burned as her mind conjured the image of Paul lying beside her, naked and beautiful in all his macho maleness. What kind of thoughts were those to have at school?

"These cables are backward. The input is in the output slot." Alex switched the cables and turned on the television.

Black and white static filled the screen and speaker.

Kendall busied herself, erasing the previous day's assignment from the big white dry-erase board. "Alex, you're such an audio-visual geek. I'm going to have to work on you to make you date-worthy."

"Girls." Alex snorted. "Who needs 'em?"

"Hey!" Kendall planted her fists on her narrow hips. "I resent that."

"You know. You're not like a girl." Alex turned away, a smirk twisting his lips.

"It's worse than I thought." Kendall shook her head at Elise. "He doesn't even know what a girl is."

Elise smiled for what felt like the first time in a long time.

"What did the police have to say about the note on your wall, Ms. Johnson?" Kendall asked, her voice stiff and unnaturally cheerful as if she was trying too hard to make the question more casual than it was.

"Kendall." Alex shot a warning glance at the girl. "You promised you wouldn't be nosy."

"I can't help asking questions. It's my nature." She smiled at Elise. "After all, someday I want to work for the FBI like Agent Fletcher."

Elise cast a glance at the door. It was closed and hopefully, no one out in the hallway could hear what was being said. "The sheriff and the FBI took pictures and dusted for fingerprints. I guess it's up to them to figure out who did it."

Kendall heaved a sigh. "Wish I could have been there when they collected the evidence."

"What, so you could ask dumb questions? Just kick her out when she gets to botherin' you too much, Ms. Johnson." Alex plugged a cable into the back of the television and the power cord into the wall. "That ought to do it."

"I've been thinking, Ms. Johnson," Kendall tipped her head to the side, a frown pressing her blond brows closer together. "Do you think the killer will come after you next? My mom won't even let me ride my bicycle down the street right now."

Elise squeezed her eyes shut to keep the ready tears from spilling. Was she doing the right thing by staying in Breuer? Was her very presence there placing all the other blond women in danger? "I don't know, Kendall."

"Why would he write that note on your wall?" the blond teen persisted.

"Kendall, shut up." Alex straightened from the back of the television and glared at his friend.

Kendall held her hands up in surrender. "What? I'm just asking."

"Maybe Ms. Johnson doesn't want to answer all your crazy questions."

"But I could be at risk, too, for all we know." She lifted the end of her blond ponytail, her brows raised.

"Yeah, and your name isn't Alice."

"Neither is Ms. Johnson's." Kendall turned her gaze back to Elise. "Your first name is Elise, isn't it? Why did the note call you Alice? I mean it sounds kinda like Alice but it's different."

"Enough, Kendall!" Alex stalked toward her.

Kendall ducked behind Elise's desk. "Leave me alone, you geek. I mean it. One step closer and I'll let you have it."

Alex took that one step and a couple more.

"You're impossible." Kendall tossed the eraser at Alex's head and missed. The eraser bounced off the front of the video player, triggering the unit to switch on.

Instead of the documentary on ancient Egypt and the pyramids, a news clip came on.

Kendall's attention shifted to the television screen. "Is that the local news channel?"

Alex returned to the set and fiddled with the buttons, changing the channels. On any other channel, he either got a blue screen or static. He hit the eject button and reloaded the disc.

Once again the screen filled with a news clip. People were standing out in the rain, wearing heavy coats and the news reporter held a microphone up to a woman clutching the hands of two small boys.

Elise's heart stumbled in her chest, her vision going blurry around the edges. She knew that woman. Knew those boys.

"Turn it off," she said, barely able to force air past her vocal cords.

Alex and Kendall moved closer to the television.

Kendall pointed at the oldest boy. "Hey, isn't that Brandon?" When she turned back to Elise, her face blanched. "Ms. Johnson, are you okay?"

Alex turned the sound up on the television, oblivious to Kendall and Elise.

"Mrs. Klaus, did you know your husband was a serial killer?"

"No." Elise's lips formed the words the woman on the screen said, the sound from the television echoing in her head as though it came from a cave.

Another reporter shoved a microphone in her face and demanded, "How could you live in the same house with a killer and not know it?"

"Please, leave us alone. I didn't have anything to do with it. I knew nothing."

The segment cut to a well-coiffed reporter. "Here in Riverton, North Dakota, with the banks of the Red

River overflowing in what's been the worst flooding since 1997, authorities are searching for the body of the Dakota Strangler, thought to have perished in a farmhouse fire. In the background, the FBI and state police are transporting the killer's wife to the police station for questioning. She claims to know nothing of her husband's connection to the deaths of five Riverton women."

The video cut to another reporter outside a school gymnasium, rain dripping off the edges of his black umbrella. "It's rumored that the Dakota Strangler's wife, Alice Klaus and her two sons are taking refuge in this evacuation shelter. Meanwhile, the body of the Dakota Strangler has yet to be recovered.

"Experts say he may never be found, his body may even be carried as far as Hudson Bay. Remnants of the house in which he'd last been seen have been found rammed against a railroad bridge crossing the Red River. No signs of the strangler himself. Authorities say the debris is too unstable to pick through at this time. With the snow melting and the continued rain, the river isn't expected to crest for another twenty-four hours."

Elise collapsed in the chair behind her desk and laid her face on the cool wooden surface. "Please, turn it off. Please." Tears spilled out of the corners of her eyes, dripping onto the calendar desk pad, smearing the ink of a note she'd jotted in a hurry.

Kendall ran for the television and hit the power

button. "Ms. Johnson." Her hand touched Elise's shoulder, but Elise could barely feel it. Her entire body had gone numb. Nightmares of reporters hounding her and the boys, the terror of outrunning the flooding in the streets, losing everything in her home and life, the accusations by the police and the press all jumbled in her mind.

"Ms. Johnson?" Alex called to her.

Elise couldn't lift her head. She moved her lips but couldn't force words to come out. I'm all right, she wanted to say but couldn't.

She wasn't all right. Nothing was all right. Her secret was out and soon all of Breuer would blame her for the deaths of women she didn't even know. Wasn't she to blame? She'd come to this town hoping to escape the death that found its way here.

"Alex, go get the principal," Kendall ordered somewhere on the other side of the haze that crowded her.

No. Elise cried out, but no sound came out. She couldn't tell the principal. With parents like Gerri Finch ready to file lawsuits, she wouldn't want that kind of scandal at her school.

"It's okay, Ms. Johnson," Kendall's voice came as if from a long way off, though she stood beside Elise. "I have the disc in my pocket. Alex and I won't tell anyone if you don't want us to."

Tainted relief flooded in on a wave of blackness and the world went dark.

* * *

PAUL STRODE into the office by eight-thirty that morning. That's where Mel cornered him.

"Tell me you have something," Paul said without the usual greeting.

"Wish I could. All I know is this guy has to be a copycat. From what we knew about Stan Klaus, he killed women who were smart because he didn't want his wife, our Elise, to get ideas about going back to school or getting smarter than him."

"We still can't rule him out." Paul pushed his hand through his hair and paced the room. "I don't like being away from her any more than we have to. My gut tells me that he'll eventually make a grab for her."

Melissa crossed her arms over her chest. "Then why are you here?"

"I have a job to do. I can't run a department from Breuer."

"Don't worry about the department right now. These guys have assignments. They're big agents who can operate independently. You said so yourself."

Paul snorted. "Everyone except maybe Agent Cain."

Mel nodded. "True. By the way, what's up with him?"

"He's been playing a disappearing act with Alvarez. I plan to get to the bottom of it tomorrow morning first thing."

"Just what you need when you have so much more on your mind." Melissa's brows rose. "Want me to check it out?"

Paul nodded. "If I'm not in first thing in the morning, tail him. See what he's up to."

"Will do." Melissa jerked her head toward the door. "But right now, you need to get back to Breuer. Elise will be biting her nails until you get there. After seeing the writing on the wall, I don't blame her."

"I know. She says she doesn't like me hanging around, but I think she feels safer when I'm there. She's more afraid people will start asking questions and find out about her past."

"It's a tough past to live with. But maybe if she would let her secret out, others around her would be on the lookout for her and keep her all the safer."

"It's hard convincing her." Paul paced the length of the office again, needing the release of exercise or hitting something, someone.

"Okay, tough guy. If you think you're needed here, why aren't you sitting at your desk pushing paper like a good supervisor should?" Melissa's words acted as a finger poked in a wound, gouging a hole in the thin veneer of reason he kept on his tightly strung control.

Sitting behind his desk would make him want to crawl right out of his skin, and damned if Melissa didn't know that. He couldn't leave Elise exposed to whoever was killing women in Breuer. "I'm going back to the school. I have a feeling there's something we're missing."

"How so?"

"The first note appeared in her box at school."

"Did you find out how it got there?"

"No. Elise didn't want me nosing around the school, alerting the staff to her situation. But I want to know how that note got in her box." Paul glanced at the paperwork piling up on his desk, a twinge of guilt eating at his gut, but not enough to stop him.

"Leave the drudgery." Melissa waved at the documents and reports. "It'll still be there once we've apprehended the Breuer Killer."

"You sound confident we'll get him soon."

"I know you," Mel said with half a smile, "and you've got that look in your eye."

"What look?"

"That look you get when you're on the trail of someone and won't let it go until you find him."

Paul shrugged. "I don't know what you're talking about." He stepped out of his office, Melissa following close on his heels. "So tomorrow, while I'm out of the office, you're going to keep up with Cain."

"Yes, sir." Mel followed him. "You know, I've never known a person Paul Fletcher couldn't get along with."

Paul strode past Cain's empty desk, noting the papers stacked in neat piles and the pens standing in an FBI coffee mug. The guy liked things orderly. If he handled his cases like he did his office, he'd be thorough. So why was he skipping out on his assigned duties? Paul made a mental note to review Cain's past cases to get to know his style more and have a talk with him in the morning. He wanted his people to work as a team.

"I have another assignment for you this afternoon. I told Elise and the boys that you would be at their house when the boys get off the school bus. She insists on being at the school for parent-teacher night."

Mel's brows rose. "What do I know about babysitting boys?"

"About as much as I do."

Mel lifted her chin. "Why don't *you* pick them up?"

"I'm going to the school to keep an eye on Elise."

Mel grinned. "You get the girl. I get the kids. One of the perks of being the boss, right? Just don't take all night, will you? I might have had plans."

"It's business," Paul insisted. Although what they'd done last night had nothing to do with business. His jeans tightened at the memory. "And you? Plans? When was the last time you had a date?"

Mel bristled. "I've had dates."

"Yeah? When?"

"Well, I could have had a date if I wasn't working." Mel's lips twisted into a wry grin. "Okay, so I haven't had a date in a while. What's it to you?"

Paul shook his head. "Just be there, will you?"

"Yes, boss." She pulled her gun from inside her jacket, checked the clip and slammed it back into the handle. "I guess I can pick up pizza on the way. Kids like pizza, don't they?"

"I don't know anyone who doesn't like pizza. Leave the stinky fish off." Paul smiled at Mel as he shot through the door leading out of the office. "Thanks, Mel. I'll let you know if we're going to be really late," he called out over his shoulder.

"Don't worry about us. I can come up with something to do with the boys."

"Just don't let them play with your weapon. And keep a close eye on Luke. He's got a habit of sneaking out the back door."

She grinned. "Check."

"I'm headed over to the coroner's office to check on our latest victim."

Melissa shook her head. "Shame about Mary Alice. She was only twenty-six. I did a background check on her boyfriend. He came up clean."

Paul snorted. "So did Stan Klaus."

* * *

"How are you feeling now?" The school nurse pressed a cool compress to Elise's forehead as she lay on the couch in the nurse's office.

Principal Ford poked her head in the door. "How is she?"

Elise pushed to a sitting position, removing the compress from her forehead. "I'm fine. Really. I should get back to my class before they destroy my room."

Principal Ford waved a hand. "I got Coach Hensley to stand in. He'll have them bench-pressing their desks to keep them busy." Her smile went a long way toward making Elise feel more at ease. The older woman nodded at the nurse. "Could we have a few minutes?"

The nurse glanced at Elise. "I'll get you a bottle of water from the lounge."

"Thanks." Elise gave the woman a wan smile, her gaze following her out the door. She wished she could escape as easily. It seemed as though the time for confession was upon her.

Principal Ford took the seat across from her and leaned forward, her hands clasped, elbows resting on her knees. "What happened?"

Elise hated lying. "I got light-headed and must have passed out."

"Elise, I know something is going on. For the past few days, you've been pale, tense and jumpy. If there's anything you'd like to tell me, maybe I can help."

If only she could. "I'm not getting much sleep." That wasn't a lie.

"Does it have to do with the man that keeps showing up around here?"

Elise's eyes widened. "What man?"

Principal Ford frowned. "The one who got Caesar to back down in your class the other day. You know, tall, blond and gorgeous. He showed us his badge in the office. FBI." She paused, giving Elise all the opportunity she needed to spill her guts.

But she just couldn't, could she? She sat silently biting her lower lip.

"Is he really your boyfriend or is he here on official business?"

Elise smiled for the first time in what felt like days, her cheeks warming at the images of what they'd done on her couch last night. Paul had obviously told the office staff he was her boyfriend to avoid generating suspicion. "He's really my b-boyfriend."

"Are the incidents with Caesar getting to you?"

"No, although that was pretty scary."

"Rumor has it he threw a brick at your car. Is that true?"

Elise shrugged. "I didn't see who threw it."

"If we find out he did it, we can press charges." The lines in Principal Ford's forehead deepened. "I don't like it when my teachers are threatened or hurt by students. I won't tolerate it. His parents have been notified that upon his return from suspension,

Caesar will be placed in the alternative center until his attitude improves."

"For his sake, I hope he returns. He needs an education. All teens need an education."

"I wish they could see that as clearly." The principal sighed. "I'm sorry. I shouldn't have lumped all the hard cases in your final class of the day. Between Caesar Valdez and Ashley Finch, you've had more than your share of trouble."

"I can handle them."

"Yeah, but you shouldn't have to handle Ashley's mother. The woman is a force to be reckoned with. If she even hints at anything resembling a threat, a reprisal or a lawsuit, you bring it straight to me."

Elise gave her boss a mock salute. "Yes, ma'am."

Principal Ford sat back in her chair, pressing her fingertips together in a steeple. "You know, Elise, I've liked you from the start. That's why I hired you. You're fresh, personable, and interested in making a difference with the students. I'd like to think you could confide in me and let me help you with any issues you might be having here at school or even outside of school. I only want to help."

Ready tears welled in Elise's eyes. For a moment she teetered on the verge of telling the other woman everything, right down to the note in her mailbox, but reason took hold, and she straightened. "Thanks, Principal Ford. I'll keep that in mind. I'm sorry for the spectacle I must have made in my classroom. I won't let it happen again."

Principal Ford rose and crossed to Elise, extending her hand to help her up from the couch. "You can't help it when you aren't feeling well. If you'd like to take the rest of the day to recuperate, please do. I can get a substitute in."

"No. I think I'll be fine. I must have skipped breakfast this morning. A little food in my stomach and I'll be fine for the rest of the day. Besides, this evening we have parent-teacher conferences scheduled. I can't miss those. Most of my students are doing well and their parents need to hear that from me."

"They'll understand if you're not feeling well. I can stand in for you."

"No, really," Elise said, "I feel like such a bother already."

"No bother. I just don't want to lose one of my shining new stars. It's hard to find high school teachers who can inspire their students and who actually care whether or not they learn."

"Thanks for your confidence in me." Elise leaned across and hugged the other woman. Maybe someday she'd share her secret with her. Just not now.

Principal Ford hugged her back, then pulled away, brushing a hand over her blazer. "Remember, my door is open if you need anything. Anything at all."

I need more than you could imagine just to survive this ordeal. "I'll remember." Elise left the room and went in search of her two pupils with a disk she needed back in her possession ASAP.

CHAPTER 14

PAUL LEFT the coroner's office within fifteen minutes of arriving with the same story as his previous visit. The victim had been choked from behind by an arm, not by an Ethernet cable.

He had a couple of places he wanted to check out today before heading to the high school to hang out with Elise during her parent-teacher conferences.

Clouds hovered over San Antonio and north into the hill country. Dark clouds laden with moisture from a system moved in from the northwest. A cool breeze promised an end to the Indian summer. Fall had officially arrived in central Texas.

Tiny droplets of rain hit his windshield as Paul left the city behind and followed the interstate northwest toward El Paso. The closer he came to the exit for Breuer, the harder the rain fell until he slowed his truck to compensate for the limited visibility and to keep from hydroplaning on the oily asphalt. Cars moved at a snail's pace through the small town, clumping at stoplights and inching forward when the light flashed a blurry green.

First stop on Paul's list was the houses surrounding Elise's. Someone might have seen a man enter her house during the day while she'd been gone to work. Surely in the old neighborhood where Elise lived, some elderly lady with a herd of cats kept a vigilant eye out her window.

Paul parked in Elise's driveway and dropped down into a puddle of water. The rain pounded against his shoulders and face. He pulled an umbrella from behind his seat and popped it open. With the rain coming in sideways, he had to tip it to keep from being soaked all over, but he couldn't help the drenching on his legs. Thank goodness he wore boots. Water ran along the sides of the curbs a foot deep, racing down the street to a drain.

The first house he came to was a modest white wood-framed house with a screened-in porch whose screens had seen better days. A rosebush climbed up the side of one screen, thorns poking holes in the metal mesh.

He pulled the screen door open and stepped onto the semi-dry porch, shaking off the rain from his umbrella. When the screen slammed behind him, a cacophony of yapping erupted from inside the little house.

He pressed the doorbell and waited. The dogs inside let up a frenzy of noise. One pushed his nose through the thin slats of aluminum blinds, its white hairy face and black button eyes shaking with eagerness to see the visitor.

Paul rang the doorbell again. Either the dogs made too much noise for the bell to be heard, or they were the only ones at home. He lifted his umbrella, ready to step off the porch when the door opened, and a white-haired old lady peeked out. "Yes?"

"Pardon me, ma'am. I'm Special Agent Paul Fletcher with the FBI. I'm hoping you can help me." He flipped his credentials out.

The woman's eyes narrowed, and her head tipped back so that she could look at his documentation through her bifocals. She opened the door a little wider. "What is it you need?"

"Your neighbor, Ms. Johnson had a break-in yesterday during the day while she was teaching at the high school. Did you happen to see any vehicles parked along the street or notice anyone enter or leave her house?"

The old woman's hand shook as she pressed it to her chest. "Oh, my. That's terrible." She glanced around as if the culprit might be lurking, waiting to break into her own home.

"Yes, ma'am." Paul wished the woman would hurry and answer his question, but knew it took time. "Did you happen to see anything?"

She shook her head. "No, no. Nothing out of the ordinary." She frowned, her head tipping to the right. "I did see one of those bug extermination trucks drive by and park several doors down around noon."

In this part of Texas, an exterminator truck was common with the number of scorpions, fire ants and sugar ants in the area. "Could you point out which house it stopped in front of?"

"The rock house three doors down, I think." She nodded. "Yes, that's the one." She smiled up at him. "That's the only vehicle I saw parked on our street during the day."

"Do you look out often?"

"Son, I sit by the window all day. I like to see what's going on since I don't get out much lately and my children only visit once or twice a year."

Paul smiled. The woman was probably lonely, watching the world pass her by out her front window.

"Do you remember the logo on the truck? Any distinguishing marks, the name?"

She shook her head. "Noooo...." Then her eyes brightened. "But it was one of those trucks with the big bug on top. Does that help?"

"No other vehicles?"

"No, that's it."

"Thank you, Mrs...?"

"Thompson. It's Mrs. Thompson." She stuck her hand through the door.

Paul took her shriveled, frail fingers and shook her hand gently. "Thank you, Mrs. Thompson. You've been a big help."

He left the covered porch, hurrying out into the rain to the house on the other side of Elise's, hoping to get a corroborating story.

After knocking on the doors of the houses on either side and in front of Elise's house with no luck, he cut through the backyard to the one behind her, where he'd seen movement the night before.

There wasn't a doorbell, so Paul opened the screen door and tapped his knuckles against the wood-paneled front door and stepped back, letting the screen door close.

At first he suspected no one was home. But then a round, dark face peered around a curtain at him from the window closest to the door. The curtain jerked closed when the viewer realized she was being viewed.

Still the door didn't open.

Impatient to be on his way, but certain someone in this house had information that could help him, he knocked louder. "This is the FBI. Please open the door."

Footsteps pattered against wooden floors inside, headed away from the front door. Whoever was inside was running away from him.

Adrenaline kicked in and Paul leaped from the porch and down into the soggy yard. He rounded the side of the house so fast, he slipped and almost fell.

A door at the rear of the house slammed shut.

Paul sped up, racing after a small figure, bundled in an old coat with the hood pulled up, making a break for the side of the house.

"Stop!" Paul yelled.

The figure glanced over his shoulder, dark eyes wide, mouth open in surprise.

Paul was almost on to the escapee when he came to a halt, shoulders sagging and breaths coming in ragged gasps. *"Por favor!"*

Paul grabbed an arm and spun the person around to discover a Hispanic woman, her eyes rounded, fearful.

"Who are you?" he asked.

She shook her head. *"No hablo Inglés."*

Just what he didn't need, to scare some illegal alien into a heart attack. He thanked his Spanish teachers from high school and college for the little bit he could speak. He switched to his broken Spanish. *"Cómo te llamas?"*

"Maria."

"Do you live there?" He pointed to the house she'd come out of.

She stared at the house and back to him, her brow furrowed.

Frustration hit hard. What were the words in Spanish? *"Vive en esa casa?"*

Her face brightened but she shook her head. "No. *Me limpio la casa.*" She moved her hand in a circular motion. "Clean *la casa.*"

Ah, Maria was the cleaning lady. Paul nodded. "*Necesito respuestas.* I need answers." He pointed to Elise's house.

Rain dripped off her face as she tipped her head back to look up into Paul's face.

He held the umbrella over her head and smiled down at her reassuringly, though he kept a firm grip on her arm. "I won't hurt you or turn you in to the authorities. I just need to know if you've seen anyone hanging around that house. *Has visto a nadie alrededor de la casa?*" He hoped he'd said that right. His luck, he was asking which way to the farm.

She shook her head. "*No, sólo a la mujer con dos niños.*"

"Were you here yesterday during the day? *Aquí fueron ayer?*"

"Si." She nodded. "*Me limpio la casa de la Señora Slater.*"

An image of little Luke talking through the bushes to his friend came to Paul's mind. Was this where George lived? "*George no vive aquí?*"

The woman nodded and she looked around as if to see if anyone else was watching her. "*Senor* George *es retrasado.*"

Paul didn't recognize the word. He shook his head. "*No entiendo.*"

She looked around as if trying to come up with a way to tell him. Finally, she shrugged and circled her finger beside her temple. "George *es muy loco.*"

Crazy? "George *es poco?*" Paul held his hand out at about Luke's height.

The woman in front of him shook her head and raised her hand to the same height as Paul.

Luke had been talking through the fence with a crazy man? What had he told him? Could he have let it slip what their last names used to be? Would the little boy have remembered?

"*Dónde está George?*" he asked.

The lady shrugged, her body drenched from the rain. She glanced longingly over her shoulder at a beat-up, rusty car parked in the gravel driveway. "I go. *Tengo que ir.*"

"Where is George?" Paul insisted.

"*En la escuela.*" She pulled free of the hand he still had on her arm and ran for the car.

At the school. George was at the school.

Before Maria had her car cranked, Paul had circled around to Elise's house and jumped into his truck. Which school? Which school was George at?

Shifting into Reverse, he spun the truck out of the driveway and shot into the street. Then he pressed the accelerator to the floor, spitting water up behind him as he blasted down Highland Street toward the high school.

Managing the turns with one hand, he slid his cell

phone open with the other and dialed Agent Bradley. "Mel, check all the bug extermination companies in Breuer and the San Antonio area for a truck scheduled for Highland Street in Breuer."

Mel didn't respond right away and then cleared her throat. "Okaayy, I'll bite. Has Elise got bug problems?"

"One of her neighbors saw an exterminator truck parked on the street yesterday. One with the bug on top of it."

"That ought to narrow it down some. I'm on it. Where are you headed now?"

"To the high school. One of Elise's neighbors works at the high school. I'm going to check him out."

"Think he was the one to leave the note in her box?"

Paul's jaw tightened. If this guy was loco as Maria indicated, there was no telling what he was capable of. "I don't know, but I plan on finding out."

Cars left the parking lot in a steady stream as the campus cleared of students. An equally steady stream of vehicles entered and filled the parking lot as parents ran or trudged through the puddles of water, hunkered beneath umbrellas to get indoors.

Paul climbed out, forgoing the umbrella since he was already soaked through to the skin. He just wanted to get to Elise.

Tables had been set up in the entrance where

parents stood in line for course schedules with class numbers for each of their children. Paul bypassed the masses and hurried toward Elise's classroom.

A dark-haired woman in a navy-blue skirt suit stepped into his path. "Agent Fletcher, is it?" She stuck her hand out, forcing him to stop and shake it. "I'm Anita Ford, the principal here at Breuer High School."

"Nice to meet you." He shook her hand, his gaze shooting past her to the hallway where Elise's classroom was located.

"Are you here on official business, or personal?" Her brows rose on her forehead, her mouth stretched in a thin line.

What was this all about? Paul shifted his full attention to Principal Ford. If he told her it was official, he'd be obliged to give her some of the details of which he wasn't prepared to impart to the woman. "Personal."

"As the principal of this school, I'm responsible for the students as well as the teachers. If this is official business, I have a right to know what it's all about."

"It's personal."

"Ms. Johnson is new to us here at Breuer, yet I like to think I treat all my teachers the same, new or tenured. If she's in any kind of trouble, I'd like to know what I can do to help."

Paul studied the woman. She seemed sincere, yet

it wasn't his place to tell her anything about Elise's past. If Elise wanted her to know, she'd have told her. "Thank you, Principal Ford. As Elise's...fiancée..." Hopefully, knowing Paul was Elise's fiancé should keep her from questioning his continued presence at the high school. "I'm relieved to know someone is looking out for her welfare."

"Fiancée?" Principal Ford's lips curved into a smile. "Is this something new?"

Paul forced a smile, hoping it looked natural and not strained. "Well as soon as I pop the question, and she says yes. You won't say anything to her, will you? I'd planned on surprising her this Friday."

Principal Ford was all grins. "You have my word. She should be in her classroom."

While he had the principal's attention, he might as well ask. "Principal Ford, do you have a man working here by the name of George Slater?"

The lady's smile softened. "Why yes. George is a janitor here at the high school." She paused. "Why do you ask?"

"Is he working now? I know he lives close to Elise, and I haven't had the opportunity to meet him."

"I'm sure he's around somewhere. He usually does the cleaning at the end of the school day after the students leave." She turned toward the office. "I can have him paged."

"That won't be necessary. I can meet him another

time." Paul smiled. "I'm more interested in seeing Elise first."

"If you're certain." She motioned toward the office. "Won't take a minute to put an announcement over the intercom system."

The offer was not Paul's idea of subtle. "No, that's okay. Maybe next time." Paul sprinted down the hallway toward Elise's room, more anxious than ever to see that she was truly all right, almost certain she would be, surrounded by parents, other teachers and students.

It gnawed at him that George was an employee of the school. In a perfect position to have access to Elise's mailbox. If the boys had somehow alerted him to their former name and circumstances, he might be the one threatening her and killing the women.

First, he'd check on Elise, then he'd find George. His gut twisted at the thought of young Luke standing at the back fence talking to the crazy man. How close to death had the boys been in their own backyard?

His cell phone rang, and he answered. "Fletcher."

"Hey, Paul. I called the bug exterminator company you mentioned before I picked up the boys. I got hold of their dispatch office in Breuer and found out something interesting."

"What's that?"

"One of the bug trucks was stolen yesterday morning before their office opened."

"Has it been located?" He couldn't imagine a truck as distinctive as one with a giant bug on it could go missing for long.

"As a matter of fact, yes. It was located a mile away in an empty lot. The police think it was kids taking it for a joy ride."

"I'll bet it was our killer."

"Did the police have the truck dusted for prints?"

"Yup. Only the regular drivers' prints showed."

Whoever had stolen it knew the ropes. Leaving no trace evidence. Paul headed toward the cafeteria. Could a high school janitor be the culprit behind such an elaborate operation? Or was Paul wasting his time and the real killer was out there preparing to strike again? He feared Elise would be his next target. Maybe Elise was right, and it was Stan Klaus. Who else would have sufficient motivation to kill others to torment her? Who else would be motivated to ultimately kill her?

"Oh, and Paul, while I was still at the office, Cain showed up for all of five minutes. I couldn't follow him because I had to pick up the boys. He looked like he was in a hurry. He left at the same time as I did. Pealed out of the parking lot in his SUV without so much as a word to me."

Paul's jaw tightened. Between protecting a woman from a crazed killer and dealing with a troubled employee, he had his share of frustrations. "I'll deal with him when I get in the office tomorrow."

* * *

ELISE SAT behind her desk with her grade sheets neatly printed, waiting for parents to show up and ask about their child's progress. For all outward appearances, she hoped she appeared calm and relaxed. While inside her stomach churned, her palms sweated, and she still felt a little light-headed.

Every time a person appeared in the doorway, Elise teetered at the edge of terror. What if Stan entered carrying an Ethernet cable, ready to take her out like he had the other women he'd killed?

Her more hopeful side watched the door, hoping Paul would step through and allay her fears. She fought the urge to call home and check on the boys. Agent Bradley had been there to see them off the bus. She'd called as soon as they arrived and again when they were safely tucked inside the house with the doors locked.

Elise would rather have skipped the parent-teacher conference night, but she feared for her job. Especially after passing out in the classroom and then lying to the principal about why.

She hadn't seen Alex and Kendall since the earlier incident. They hadn't shown up for class, either. She'd called their homes and left a message, but they hadn't checked in. Now, not only did she have to worry about her own children, but she was also worried about her students. The burden of her situation weighed heavily on her.

Just when she thought things couldn't get worse, Gerri Finch walked in, her three-inch stilettos clicking sharply against the tiles. Ashley followed her mother, her head down, her cheeks pale.

"I've had about all I can take of this school, Ms. Johnson." Gerri plopped her Gucci bag on Elise's desk and planted her hands on her hips. "My daughter will be at the cheer competition on Saturday, do you understand? If she's not, I'll hold you responsible and do my best to have you fired."

All the frustration, fear and anger that had built up over the past couple of days rocketed up inside Elise. She stood, heat rising up her neck into her face and all the way to her scalp. "Mrs. Finch." Elise sucked in a deep breath in hope of calming her rising fury. "Ashley is responsible for whether or not she performs on Saturday. She needs to understand that there are consequences for her actions. And you, as her parent, should know that and provide the guidance she so desperately needs and obviously isn't getting."

"Mom, leave it alone." Ashley grabbed her mother's arm and tried to pull her away from Elise's desk. "So, I'll miss one competition. The world won't end."

"Shut up, Ashley. You'll be there if I have to file a lawsuit against this school and particularly against this teacher."

Ashley's face reddened and she shot a helpless glance at Elise. "But I don't want you to sue the school. I like it here. I have friends."

Mrs. Finch's cheeks flushed an unbecoming beet-red. "I said shut up! If you hadn't kept your mouth shut in the first place, and gotten to class on time, you wouldn't be in this situation. Let go of me!" Gerri Finch jerked her arm loose and raised her hand as if to strike her daughter.

Ashley flinched and backed away, color draining from her face.

Elise gasped. "Mrs. Finch!"

"Don't." Paul's deep voice penetrated the woman's rage and halted her hand in midair.

Relief washed over Elise, and she rushed across the room and into his open arms.

Gerri's hand remained frozen, hovering over her daughter's head, her breath coming in ragged gasps. "You have to be at the competition."

"Why, Mom?" Ashley's color came back, tears filling her eyes. "*You're* the one who wanted me to cheer. *You're* the one who made me go to all those gymnastic lessons. Did you ever ask me what I wanted? I hate gymnastics. I hate cheering!"

Gerri stared at her raised hand and back at her daughter. Her hand dropped to her side, her shoulders sagging. "I wanted you to have all the things I didn't."

"But I don't want them, Mom. I just want to go to

school, graduate and get the hell out of the house. Away from my crazy mother who won't quit embarrassing me in front of the entire school."

Gerri's own eyes glazed as she stared across at her daughter as if for the first time. "But you're my baby. I love you."

"Just let me live *my* life, *my* way." Ashley's face softened. "Come on, Mom. Let's get out of here."

"One question before you leave." Paul stood between them and the doorway. "Did either one of you throw a brick at Ms. Johnson's car yesterday around four o'clock?"

Ashley and Gerri Finch both blinked.

"I was getting a facial at that time," Gerri answered.

"I have cheer practice every day after school," Ashley said. "Someone threw a brick at your car?" The young woman turned to Elise, her forehead creased in a frown. "I might have been mad at you, but not that mad."

"It wasn't them." A tall Hispanic man with a heavy accent, pushed Caesar Valdez through the door, his hand clenched around the boy's collar. "Tell them."

Caesar, his chin tucked into his chest, scuffed his toe on the tile. "I threw the brick, Ms. Johnson. I'm sorry."

Elise couldn't stop the gasp, but when Paul tensed beside her, she put out a hand to hold him back. She nodded at Ashley and her mother. "I'll see you in class tomorrow, Ashley?"

Ashley's gaze shot from Caesar to Elise and back. She looked like she wanted to stay for the show.

"You two have a lot to talk about at home." Elise followed them to the door, ushering them out. "Goodbye, Ashley, Mrs. Finch." She closed the door and turned to Caesar, her heart pounding against her chest. "Surely you knew that throwing a brick at my car could hurt me, maybe even kill me."

"I wanted to hurt you." He threw back his head and glared at her. "I'm tired of school. It's a waste of time. If I wasn't stuck in class, I could get out and get a job now."

"A job paying no more than minimum wage for the rest of your life. You can do better than that. You can do better than me." The man beside Caesar stuck out his hand. "Raul Valdez. Caesar's father."

The man's large paw engulfed Elise's small hand, the rough calluses from hard physical labor scraping against her softer skin.

"What Caesar isn't saying is that he's having trouble with all of his classes, and he wants to give up," his father said. "He wants to quit school, so he's acting up in all his classes, hoping they'll kick him out."

Elise stepped forward. "Caesar, you can't give up."

"When will I ever use stupid history? How will it help me get a job?"

"There are teachers all over this school who want to help you. All you have to do is be willing to try. We have after-school tutoring for every subject. I have early morning help in my class. Some of my students tutor."

"I spend enough time in this hellhole. Why would I want to spend more?"

"Because you're an intelligent young man and you can do anything you set your mind to," Elise said.

"I'm not. I barely get by in this class and I'm failing in others."

Elise laid a hand on his arm. "I'll help you."

"Why do you want to help me?" He stared at the hand on his arm. "I threw a freakin' brick at your car."

"Yes, you did." Elise's lips pressed into a line. "And you'll pay to have it replaced. But to keep me from filing a report to the police, you'll come to my class early every morning and study with me. Bring whatever subject you're having difficulties with, and I'll help."

Caesar stared into Elise's eyes, his brown ones brooding and suspicious. "Why?"

"Because, though you might think all teachers are here to torture you, we do care about our students' futures." Elise smiled and removed her hand from his arm. "And once upon a time, I didn't think I could do anything with my life," she said softly. "But I was wrong."

All the years of marriage to Stan Klaus. How he'd controlled her life, how he'd insisted on her being a stay-at-home mom. Not so much for the sake of her boys, but because he didn't want her to be smarter than him. He didn't want her to go out into the world and be more important than he was.

"I want you to be successful, Caesar. I want you to know you can do better than pushing people around who are smaller than you. But you need to know that I won't tolerate you threatening me or any other student ever again."

"I understand if you want to press charges. He deserves it." Caesar's father glared at his son. "I also want you to understand that I raised him better, and he will make it up to you if you give him a chance. I'll see to that."

Elise raised her hands palms up. "It's completely up to Caesar. Will you show up every day and work hard without complaint?"

Caesar sucked in a deep breath and let it out, thinking about her offer for a long minute. Finally, he shrugged. "Okay." His father nudged him hard with his elbow. "Yes, ma'am."

Caesar's mouth twisted and he rubbed his ribs. "Yes, ma'am."

"I'll see you in the morning, then." Elise grinned. "And Caesar, bring your books."

The Valdezes left her room and Elise stared after them.

Paul gripped her shoulders and leaned her against him. "Tough day?"

"You have no idea." She turned and buried her face in his chest, her arms wrapping around his waist. "I didn't think it could get more stressful. But it continues to do so."

"I understand you were under the weather earlier?" He tipped her chin up and studied her face.

Elise could stand there forever, melting into his gaze, warming her body with the heat from his. "I had a gift left in my DVD player." Before she could fill him in on what had happened earlier that day, a parent arrived at her door.

* * *

Elise forced a smile, gave the parent an update on her student and thanked her for coming.

Paul stood in a far corner, staring at a map on the wall, probably trying to be inconspicuous.

It wasn't working. Paul's broad shoulders and tough-guy stance made him hard to ignore. Elise's gaze slipped to him more than she intended.

As soon as the mother left the room, Paul was beside her. "What gift?"

"A video of the news reports filmed two years ago after the Dakota Strangler went missing."

Paul's fingers gripped her arms. "Where is the DVD?"

"I don't have it. Alex and Kendall hid it before the principal could see it. I haven't seen them since. And frankly, I'm worried."

"Can you leave now?"

"I'm supposed to stay until seven o'clock, but I guess I could ask the principal to fill in for me." She glanced at the clock. "Could you give me a few minutes to put my papers in order?"

"Yes, I have something I want to check on. Promise you won't step outside this room until I get back?"

Elise smiled. If it had been Stan, he'd have demanded that she do exactly as he instructed. With Paul, he made it sound like she had a choice. "Yes, I promise to stay right here until you get back. Where are you going?"

"Do you know George, the janitor?"

Elise remembered seeing the janitors in the hallway, but she didn't stick around after school long enough to get to know them. "No, not really, why?"

"Did you know that one of them lives behind you?"

Her eyes widened. "Really?"

"I think it's the same George that Luke has been talking to through the fence."

"Is that a bad thing?" Elise asked.

"I don't know, but I wanted to check him out while I was here."

"I think the janitors are here at this time. They

usually come in after school gets out. I think the male janitor takes the cafeteria and the woman works the front offices." She shrugged. "I try not to stay late very often. If I do, the boys are with me."

Paul nodded. "I'll be back in a minute. I want to talk to both janitors."

Elise smiled. "I'll be here."

Paul left the room.

A few more parents wandered in. Elise gave them grade reports and talked about their students, while her mind wandered to what Paul was up to.

Could the janitor be the one terrorizing her and the women of Breuer? A janitor? Had Luke told him what their last names used to be? Elise didn't think he would have remembered.

After what seemed a long time of watching her door, meeting with parents and generally gnashing her teeth, Elise straightened her desk, grabbed her purse and keys and headed for her classroom door. She'd stop by the principal's office and let Principal Ford know she was leaving early.

As she stepped into the hallway, a loud boom shook the entire school. Elise dropped to the floor and covered her head as a blast of smoke and dust blew through the hallway.

CHAPTER 15

PAUL SLAMMED BACK against the concrete walls of the building, the air knocked from his lungs. When the explosion rocked the school, he'd been on his way to the gymnasium in a separate building, where a teacher had said she'd last seen George Slater.

Adrenaline got his heart going and he sucked in a long, deep breath, restoring oxygen to his brain. Then, he was on his feet and running through the darkened hallways. His path snarled with screaming women and crying children. Unable to move through them, he located an exit and helped the frightened parents outside. Cloud-cloaked skies made nightfall before its time. The rain continued to pour down in torrents, soaking his view and blinding him to the darkness. Had Elise made it out? Were there others trapped in the building?

Bright flames licked through the roof of the

building in the direction of the gymnasium. Paul ducked back inside. He had to get to Elise.

"Help me, please!" A woman grabbed his arm, coughed and pulled him toward the smoke. "My son was in the gymnasium getting a soda from the machine. I think he's still in there."

"What's his name?"

"Michael."

"Paul? Paul? Is that you?" Elise materialized out of the smoke, her wool scarf pulled up over her nose and eyes, a flashlight shaking in her hands. "Oh, thank God!"

"Elise, get this woman outside. I'm going back in."

"I'm going with you."

"No, it will be faster if I go without you. Please take this woman outside."

"My son is in there. I have to find him." The woman headed toward the gymnasium, tears streaming from her eyes.

Elise grabbed her arm and held tight. "You have to let Paul find him. He's trained in this kind of thing." She handed him the flashlight she'd been holding and unwound the scarf from her neck. "Take these and hurry."

Paul wrapped the scarf around his nose and mouth, hunkered low and ran down the hallway toward the gymnasium.

He shined his light in the open doorways, searching for victims too scared or disoriented to find their way out. When he made it to the gymnasium, the smoke was getting so thick his eyes burned, and the scarf was doing little to keep the smoke from his lungs. He coughed and yelled through the fabric, "Michael!"

Was that a groan? Paul closed his eyes to the smoke and listened.

Another groan.

Paul ducked low and peered beneath the layer of rising smoke, shining his flashlight across the floor. He spotted what looked like two lumps of rags near the vending machines. One moved.

"Michael!"

"Over here," a scratchy voice called out, followed by coughing.

Paul crawled on his hands and knees toward the sound, tucking the scarf securely around his face. "Gotta get out of here."

"No, duh." More coughing led Paul to the downed boy.

"Are you hurt?"

"My ankle hurts." A coughing fit racked his body. When he tried to stand, he yelped and dropped to the floor. "I can't walk."

"Grab around my neck and hold on." Paul hooked his arm around the boy's back and lifted.

"Wait. There's someone else over there."

Paul glanced over his shoulder at the limp form on the floor. "I can only move one of you at a time."

"It's..." Michael coughed. "The janitor."

The very person Paul had been looking for. "First, let's get you out, then I'll come back for him."

Running low to the ground, Paul hauled Michael out of the gymnasium and down the hall toward the exit, the boy hopping on his good foot. One of the parents met them close to the exit and took over. Paul, his lungs burning, blinking back the smokey tears in his eyes, jogged back into the building. He found his way to the gymnasium, the smoke nearly overwhelming him. He slid to his knees and crawled the rest of the way to the man lying on the floor near the vending machines.

He was a full-sized adult, weighing as much if not more than Paul. Fighting the effects of the smoke, Paul grabbed the man underneath his arms and dragged him back the way he'd come, one slow, agonizing floor tile at a time.

By the time he reached the hallway leading toward the exit, other hands took over. Firefighters in yellow jackets and oxygen masks lifted the man off the floor and carried him the rest of the way out of the building. Another fireman hooked an arm beneath Paul's and hefted him to his feet, leading, half-carrying him out into the rain, where they laid him on the soggy ground.

Blessedly cool water pelted his face, washing away a layer of soot and smoke, clearing the raw stinging sensation from his eyes. Paul dragged clean, fresh air into his lungs, coughed and sat up. "Elise." He stared around at the crowd of emergency responders tending to the fire and the injured.

Where was Elise? When he tried to stand, his legs shook and he staggered, landing on his knees.

"Here." An EMT shoved an oxygen mask over his face. "Breathe."

Paul didn't want to breathe, he wanted to find Elise. What if the explosion had been intentional? What if the killer had set it off to confuse everyone?

He sucked in a deep breath and handed the mask back to the technician. "Where's the guy I pulled out of there?"

"They're loading him into the ambulance over there." The EMT pointed at a group of medical technicians shoving a gurney in through the back door of a waiting ambulance.

While watching out for Elise, Paul lurched to his feet and caught the door before it closed. "Is he alive?"

"Yeah, you know this guy?" one of the techs asked. "You a relative or something?"

"No. I'm just concerned. I got him out of the gymnasium."

"Oh, well thanks. You probably saved his life. The principal was concerned about him, said he would need family around when he came to."

"Why?" Paul asked.

"She said that he is mentally disabled, and he'll be scared. I was hoping you were family."

Paul backed away and the door to the ambulance closed. The lights flickered on, and the siren flared.

George was mentally disabled.

Which took him off the list of suspects, although he could have been tricked into dropping a letter into Elise's mailbox, if he could read well enough to know which was hers.

Back to square one. Paul forced himself to think through the facts. The M.O. wasn't exactly the same on the killings. The method was close, but not exact. Even if it were the Dakota Strangler, how would he have found Elise? Did he stalk Brenna, Elise's sister, and glean information from her phone records?

Brenna was too good a cop to let it slip where her sister was. If not from Brenna, how did someone learn the whereabouts of a person in the witness protection program?

An insider?

Paul's heart stuttered in his chest. Who had sufficient motivation to kill women other than the original Dakota Strangler? Someone angry at Elise? He shook his head. She'd done nothing. Her husband was the killer, not her. If it were an insider, could it be someone involved in the original case? The FBI agents on the case had been Paul, Melissa and Nick. Brenna had been working for the state on the crimes.

He'd trust everyone from the team with his life and Elise's.

Then who? Someone who wanted the Dakota Strangler to be alive again. But why? Who was he really after?

Paul filtered through the crowd of emergency workers and victims, frantically searching for the woman he was as near as he'd ever come to falling in love with. Where was Elise?

* * *

THE FIREFIGHTERS HAD FORCED all onlookers back to clear the way for them to perform their search and rescue routine.

Unlike so many others, Elise had been fortunate enough to escape her classroom with her purse and keys.

She strained to see over the shoulders of the parents searching for their children and past the firefighters running hoses to the fire. The cool rain helped to keep it from spreading quickly, but it also chilled her to the bone. Still, she stood in the rain and waited for Paul to emerge from the smokey building.

Her cell phone vibrated in her purse against her leg. She scrambled through her purse to find it. When she did and read the text message on the screen, her blood ran colder than the air outside.

Where's Paul? Luke is missing. It was from Melissa Bradley.

Elise ran to the nearest fireman. "Did Paul Fletcher come out of there yet?"

"Lady, I couldn't tell you if the Pope stepped out right now. Please stay back while the emergency personnel work."

Desperate to find Paul, Elise placed a hand on the fireman's arm. "But I have to find him. It's an emergency."

"No kidding about the emergency. You and half a dozen other people are looking for loved ones. If you don't stay back, we can't do our jobs and find them."

"But—" She backed away, her heart racing in her chest. She couldn't wait for Paul. She had to do something. Luke could be in trouble. If Stan really was alive, he could have snatched the boy and run with him.

A sob welled up in her throat. She was torn, afraid to leave before making sure the man she was seriously in danger of losing her heart to made it out of the burning building alive. Paul was a grown man, there were emergency personnel crawling all over the place. They'd make sure he got out okay.

In the meantime, her son was missing. A defenseless little boy against a crazed killer didn't stand a chance. Agent Bradley had her hands tied, watching over Brandon. She couldn't go after Luke when Elise's other son was in danger as well.

Elise made the decision. She yanked a piece of paper from a pad in her purse and scribbled a note on it, telling Paul where she'd gone and why. She handed the note to the first policeman she came to. "Please make sure FBI Agent Paul Fletcher gets this note."

"Lady, I don't know who he is." He tried to hand it back to her. "Give it to him yourself."

"I can't. He's tall and blond and he went back into that building to save a woman's son. When he comes out, give him this." She shoved the note into the man's hand, refusing to let him give it back. "It's a matter of life and death."

With one last glance toward the building, Elise ran toward her little gray car that had been delivered with a new windshield early that afternoon. Thank goodness she had rescued her purse from her classroom. She dialed Paul's number. The connection went directly to his voicemail. *Damn.* With no other recourse, she left a message and climbed into her car.

Rain dripped off the end of her nose and down inside her jacket. The cold penetrated her clothing, sinking all the way to her heart. If someone had taken Luke, she wouldn't begin to know where to look. Tears filled her eyes, making it impossible to drive. She blinked them back, fiercely determined to be strong for her sons, strong for Paul and most of all strong for herself. She couldn't fail Luke.

Elise inched her way out of the parking lot,

careful to avoid emergency vehicles and gawkers. "Move, please," she said aloud, though no one could hear her with the driving rain and emergency sirens. She slammed her palm against her steering wheel, fear for her son making her want to slam her foot down on the accelerator and fly home. The longer Luke was missing, the farther away the killer could get with him.

As soon as the roadway cleared ahead of her, Elise dropped her foot to the floor, urging her little car beyond the posted speed limits, only slowing for stop signs to avoid wrecking and further delaying her arrival at her house. Several times, she hydroplaned on the slick roads, her heart in her throat as she slid close to mailboxes only to right herself and press forward.

Melissa's red pickup stood in the driveway outside Elise's house. Skidding in next to it, she slammed on her brakes, shoved the shift into Park and leaped out.

Agent Bradley met her at the door. "Where's Paul?" She stared closer at Elise. "What happened?"

"There was an explosion at the school. I left. Paul was still helping people out of the building." Elise pushed past Melissa. "Where's Brandon?"

"I'm here." Brandon stood in the middle of the living room, his backpack on, fully clothed in jeans, jacket and shoes.

"How long has Luke been gone?" Elise asked.

"Around fifteen minutes, twenty tops. I tried to call you as soon as I discovered he was missing."

Elise dropped to her haunches next to her oldest son. "Are you all right?"

He nodded, solemnly. "We have to find Luke. It's raining outside." Brandon waved a hand toward the door, his brow furrowed into a frown that was too heavy for a boy his age. "Luke gets scared when there's thunder."

"I know, I know, honey. We'll find him." She hugged Brandon, straightened and turned back to Melissa. "How did he get out of the house?"

"I went to answer my phone, and the next thing I knew, he'd gone out the back door."

"He went to find George. He wanted to show him a picture of the puppy he wants to get." Brandon's eyes filled. "It's all my fault. If I hadn't shown him the picture, he'd still be here."

"It's not your fault, Brandon. You can't keep an eye on Luke all the time. He's fast and determined to do what he wants to do." Elise recognized the same guilt in Brandon as she felt herself. She should have been here—she should have guarded her sons.

"But I'm supposed to be the man of the house." The tears spilled out of the corners of his eyes. "I didn't save him. Now he's going to die."

Elise's heart burned in her chest. "Listen to me, Brandon. Luke is not going to die. And this is not your fault. Luke shouldn't have left the house. He knows better." If anyone was at fault, it was her. She shouldn't have left her children, knowing a killer was loose, threatening her and her family.

"I'm sorry, Elise. I turned my back for a moment. I never thought he'd leave the house."

Elise wanted to yell at Melissa, wanted to scream and cry, but she couldn't. All of this was her fault. She should have moved farther away, maybe to Mexico or South America. Some place where no one could find out about her past and no one could trace her or her children. Was there such a place? She shook her head. "The important thing right now is to find Luke."

"Right. Now that you're here, I can get out and start canvassing the neighborhood. The sooner we find him the better. Problem is that I can't wait for Paul to get back to protect you two."

"We'll be fine, just go."

"Lock the door. Don't let anyone inside."

"But I can't just stand here and do nothing. I have to look for Luke, too. I can't stay locked in my house while my son is in danger."

"You have *two* sons, Elise. You need to take care of this one." She shot a pointed look at Brandon who scrubbed at his eyes, trying to act brave when he was probably falling apart inside.

Elise ached for her oldest son. He shouldn't have been through so much in his short life. She was lucky he wasn't more screwed up than he was. "Okay. We'll wait until Paul gets here. But then we have to find him."

Melissa ran for the door, shrugging into a waterproof jacket, her cowboy boots, tapping against the entrance tiles. "I'll have my cell phone. Call if you hear or see anything."

The screen door slammed behind Melissa.

Elise stood at the door for a moment, staring out into the cool, wet night, her heart squeezing in her chest. She strained to hear over the water dripping off the eaves. Elise listened hard, hoping to hear her young son's voice calling out to her from the shadows.

A small hand tugged the back of her wet jacket. "Mom, we have to go out and look for Luke."

She turned to stare down into her son's face. "Oh, darling, we have to wait here in case he comes home. What if he found his way home and no one was here to let him in?"

"He would already be home if he could get here. Luke needs us." Brandon pulled her hand, urging her toward the door. "I know his hiding places. I can find him."

"It's dark and wet out there, baby. I can't risk losing you, too." And she couldn't risk exposing Brandon to the killer.

"But Luke is part of our family. We won't be a family without him."

Elise dropped to her knees and hugged her son. "I know, honey, I know."

The cell phone in her pocket rang, the vibration startling her. She jumped to her feet and fumbled in her jacket to locate the device. It could be Melissa, she could have found Luke.

Unknown Caller displayed on the screen. Cold fingers of dread clutched her chest and squeezed. She pressed the talk button and held the phone to her ear, her hand shaking. "Hello?"

"Mama, I'm scared." Luke's plaintive cry echoed in her ear. He sniffed and called out in a little above a whisper, "I want to come home."

"Luke?" Elise clutched the phone, wishing she could reach through and hold onto her son. "Luke?" She could hear him crying in the distance, but she could do nothing to comfort him.

"He's fine as long as you do exactly as you're told." That familiar mechanical voice sounded in her ear.

"Who is this? Where have you taken my son?"

"Shut up and listen or the kid dies."

Elise took a breath and forced a calm she didn't feel. The killer had her son. If she stood any chance of seeing him again, she had to do as he said. "What do you want?"

"I want you." The three words echoed in her head as though bouncing off the walls of a long tunnel. Silence followed when all she could hear was the blood pounding in her eardrums.

"Don't hurt Luke. I'll do whatever you say." Cold determination settled over her. She avoided looking down at Brandon, knowing he understood more than any eight-year-old should and would get the gist of her conversation.

"Good girl. Drive out to the Guadalupe River Bridge on Highway 474 north of town. Luke and I will be waiting for you there. If you tell anyone, if anyone follows you, I'll kill him. Do you understand? I'll kill your son."

The nightmare had returned. Her husband's legacy had followed her to Texas and turned on her sons. She couldn't run from it, she couldn't hide. She had to stand and fight to win her freedom from the terror, to save her sons from their father's horrifying past. She'd been a doormat to Stan Klaus, someone he could walk all over and abuse mentally, if not physically. She wouldn't let anyone do that to her again. And she wouldn't let anyone threaten her sons and get away with it.

Her shoulders thrown back, her head held high, she knew what she had to do. "I understand. I'll be there. Alone."

CHAPTER 16

PAUL COULDN'T FIND HER. He'd searched the thinning crowd several times but couldn't find Elise. He turned to the parking lot and searched through the cars to find her little gray sedan with the Minnesota Vikings bumper sticker. It had been there earlier when he'd arrived at the school. The automobile service had gone the extra mile, had the car's windshield fixed and delivered the car to her school today, as good as new.

Of all the times for an automobile service to be efficient. Why couldn't they have taken more time? Then Elise would have been stranded at the high school, and she would have had to rely on him to get her where she needed to go. The only place she could be was back home. Something must be wrong with the boys. The other more disturbing thought, he brushed aside, refusing to entertain.

The killer had *not* taken Elise. He couldn't have.

Paul dug in his jacket pocket to find his cell phone. He cursed at the broken screen. He must have fallen on it. He tried calling Elise but couldn't even get a dial tone. His cell phone was dead.

Mounting dread pressed against his chest. The explosion in the high school hadn't been an accident. The firefighters might not know that yet, but Paul did. It had been a diversion. A chance for someone to lure Elise away from the grounds, maybe even kidnap her.

Without a cell phone, Paul had only one choice; he had to get to Elise's house. Worst-case scenario, he'd find Melissa and a telephone. Best case, Elise had gotten tired of waiting for him and had gone home. He'd find her there tucking Luke and Brandon into bed, kissing them good night, just like every other night. Just like normal.

This day had been anything but normal so far; why should that change now? Paul inched his truck around the emergency vehicles and out into the street, where he slammed the gas pedal to the floorboard.

The two miles to Elise's little house on Highland passed too slowly and filled him with terrifying possibilities. What if Elise had been taken by the killer? What if Melissa and the boys were hurt? What if Paul was too late?

Even without a firm suspect, Paul couldn't believe

the Dakota Strangler had survived the fire and flood. His gut told him to look elsewhere. But who would want to hurt Elise and why? The witness had reported a black SUV leaving the bridge access road. An image of a black SUV popped into his mind as clearly as if he'd seen it. And he had, but where?

Then he remembered. One had been parked next to his truck in the parking lot of the Bureau building the day this all began.

Paul shook his head. No, it was just a coincidence. There were hundreds of black SUVs all over San Antonio.

Could someone in the Bureau have gotten the information of Elise's whereabouts? Someone who knew how the witness protection program worked.

He skidded around the corner a block away from Highland Street and almost ran into Melissa on foot, waving at him from the sidewalk.

Jamming his foot on the brake, he slid to a halt, popping the automatic door locks open.

Melissa slid in, rain dripping off her jacket onto the seat, breathing hard, her face screwed into a scared frown. "Luke is gone."

"What?" The bottom fell out of Paul's stomach. Luke was a bright, active little boy with an imagination and charm that had endeared him to Paul. He'd be proud to have such a little boy as his son. "How did that happen?"

Agent Bradley shrugged, shaking her wet head. "I

don't know. One minute he was there, the next, he was gone."

"Does Elise know?" How would she react? God, she needed someone to be with her. Paul needed to be with her.

"I called her as soon as I realized he was gone. She came within fifteen minutes."

A cold tingling sensation began at the back of Paul's neck and snaked its way down his spine. "Where is Elise now?"

"I left Elise and Brandon at the house while I searched the neighborhood. I called the police, but they're tied up at the school fire. Geez, Paul, why haven't you answered your phone?" She took a deep breath, her brown hair hanging in lank, wet ropes along the sides of her face. "I lost the kid, Paul. I can't believe I lost the kid. It was just like you said, he slipped out the back door when I wasn't looking."

Paul took the corner onto Highland Street too fast for the rain-slicked road. The rear tires fishtailed on the slippery surface and straightened.

Light shone on Elise's porch, but that didn't make Paul feel any better. Not until he saw Elise, Brandon and Luke all standing in their living room, safe, well and happy, would he feel better.

Mel's red truck stood in the driveway. Alone.

"Oh, God, her car's gone. I shouldn't have left her." Mel jumped from Paul's truck before it came to a complete halt and ran for the house. Paul wasn't far behind and caught her as she reached the door. It was unlocked and easily swung open when given a gentle push.

Lights blazed from all the rooms in the house, but it stood eerily silent. A few toy cars littered the floor, lying neglected and forgotten.

Paul ran from room to room, knowing before he completed his search that he wouldn't find them. He'd let Elise and her boys down. He hadn't been there to stop a crazed killer from taking them from their home.

"What now?" Melissa stood by the door, her face glum, her lips pressed into a tight line.

"Ms. Johnson!" A voice drifted through the open door. "Ms. Johnson?" The sound of light metal clashing against concrete was followed by Elise's students, Kendall and Alex, bursting through the door.

"Where's Ms. Johnson?" Kendall blurted, then sucked in a deep breath. Her hair clung to her cheeks in wet strands and water ran in rivulets down her jacket onto the tile entrance.

"She's missing," Paul answered, his tone as flat as his heart.

"Oh, no! We were afraid someone might hurt her." Kendall pulled at Alex's coat. "Give them the disk."

Alex frowned and jerked away from Kendall's hands. "Let me unzip my jacket, will ya?" He ripped the zipper down and a DVD fell to the floor.

"What's this?" Paul grabbed the disk.

"It's the disk that was in Ms. Johnson's audio-visual equipment this morning. It had film clips from news reports of the Dakota Strangler on it."

"Why do you have it?" Paul carried it to the DVD player above the television and fed it into the machine.

Kendall's cheeks reddened. "When Ms. Johnson passed out in her room, we got scared. We promised we wouldn't let anyone else see the disk, so we took it."

"Then the bright one here," Alex jerked his thumb toward Kendall, "decided we should see if we could come up with some clues as to who put it there."

"We just *know* it had something to do with the writing on the wall in Ms. Johnson's house, so we spent the day asking around—"

Alex rolled his eyes. "Ditching class, you mean."

"I wanted to find out if anyone saw someone coming in or out of Ms. Johnson's room. I couldn't go to class, knowing someone wanted to scare her like that. Heck, I was scared, too."

"And did you?" Melissa asked. "Find anyone who saw something?"

Kendall's face brightened. "Yeah, we sure did." She grinned at Alex. "Thanks to Alex, who can speak fluent Spanish."

Alex shrugged, his cheeks turning a ruddy red. "No problem."

"There's a cafeteria worker who doesn't speak English very well," Kendall said. "Anyway, she confessed to letting a man in the cafeteria door early this morning and also two days ago."

Paul grabbed Alex by the arms, past his level of endurance. Past the need for patience. "Did she give a description of the man?"

"Not much of one. Brown hair, brown eyes, so high." Alex raised his hand to somewhere between Melissa's and Paul's height. "Could be anyone."

Kendall nudged Alex. "Oh, but when Alex asked her why she let him in when it was against the rules, she got all shaky. We had to promise we wouldn't tell anyone before she'd tell us why." Kendall frowned. "I guess we're gonna have to break that promise."

Alex picked up where Kendall stopped. "She said the man threatened her. He said he'd fixed her background check and could unfix it if she didn't help him."

Kendall looked to Alex. "We weren't sure what that meant, but anything could be important in a case, right? Even the smallest detail?" She gave Paul a weak smile.

Paul's glance clashed with Melissa's. "What does Cain drive?"

Melissa frowned. "He bought a black SUV about the same time as I bought my truck."

His chest tightened. "A witness saw a black SUV leaving the scene of the second murder. It all makes sense now." Paul's eyes squeezed shut. "This isn't about Elise at all. It's about me. Why didn't I see it?"

"Who would have thought someone on our own team would be behind this? We're supposed to be the good guys." Melissa snorted. "I knew there was a reason I didn't like that guy."

Paul pulled his thoughts together. "Have Brian run the GPS tracker on Cain's cell phone."

Thank goodness each of their department cell phones was equipped with the ability to track them via the global positioning system. He didn't know where Elise had gone or how long it would take to find her. But he did know Cain wouldn't hesitate to kill again. Why hadn't he heeded the warning signs? Why hadn't he put a tail on Cain when he first suspected something fishy?

Melissa placed a hand over his forearm, the other holding her cell phone to her ear. "You can't blame yourself."

Paul's back teeth ground together. He sure as hell could. "Tell Brian to hurry."

* * *

WHEN ELISE REACHED the bridge spanning the Guadalupe River, she slowed, scanning the bridge for Luke and his captor.

"Where is he, Mom? Where's Luke?" Brandon's breath warmed her shoulder.

"Get down!" She hadn't wanted to leave Brandon alone in case the killer had set up yet another trap to capture her other son. She hadn't wanted to alert Melissa or the police and give the killer a reason to force his hand and kill Luke. Instead, she'd made Brandon promise to stay low and if anything bad happened, he should run as fast as he could. She'd given him her cell phone and made him promise not to use it until he absolutely had to.

Brandon ducked down below the seat. "I'm scared."

"Me, too, baby. Me too." The rain had slackened but still came down in a heavy drizzle, keeping the highway slick, with water flowing into the ditches.

On the opposite side of the bridge, she found a dirt road that led down to the river twenty feet below. Already, weather reports on the radio had indicated the river had risen well above its normal levels. Usually no more than a meandering stream, the Guadalupe River was known to rise up over the bridge twenty or more feet above the riverbed. Elise, being new to the area, had yet to witness what the locals called the forces of nature in action. She hoped she wasn't about to capture her first glimpse.

Elise wasn't sure her car could make it down and back up the muddy road. Unwilling to risk Brandon's safety any more than she had, she parked her car at the top and turned in her seat. "Brandon."

"Yes, Mama." His head popped up over the back of

the seat, his eyes wide and shiny in the lights from the dashboard.

"I'm going to get Luke." She touched the cell phone in his hand. "If I don't come back in ten minutes, you find Agent Fletcher's name on my favorites list and call him. Tell him you're at the Guadalupe River Bridge on Highway 474."

"Why don't you call him now?"

"The man who has Luke said I shouldn't call anyone, or he'd hurt Luke."

"Then why do you want me to call?"

"In case Luke and I don't come back, you need to get help for yourself."

"I want to go with you."

"You can't. As the man of the house, you need to do what I tell you."

His lip trembled. "I don't want to be the man of the house. I want to go with you."

"Please, Brandon. Please do as I say. Wait ten minutes and call Paul. He'll help." She reached for the door handle, peering through the windshield into the dark.

Tires had spun up the mud on the tracks leading down to the river, but she couldn't see what awaited her there. She turned back to her oldest son. "Brandon, if anyone but me comes back up here, you get out of the car and run as fast as you can away from here before you call Paul. Do you understand?"

He nodded, a tear trickling down his cheek.

"I love you, Brandon. And I promise that I'll do my best to come back. With your brother." She leaned across the seat and hugged him, pressing a kiss to his forehead. "I love you so much."

Elise dug a flashlight out from beneath her seat and got out of the car. She slipped and caught herself on the door, fumbling to keep the light in her hand. After righting herself, she set off down the muddy track to the river and her youngest son. Rain blurred her vision, mixing with the tears welling in her eyes. Blinking only seemed to make it worse.

She couldn't go soft now. Luke needed her. Brandon needed her and Luke to return. Her oldest son would never forgive himself if something happened to either one of them. Failure was *not* an option. She slipped in the mud. Water filled her shoes and soaked her stockings. As usual, hindsight was twenty-twenty, and she should have changed into tennis shoes before she'd left the house. In the ballet flats she'd worn to school that day, she got little traction in the miniature river flowing down the hill in the rutted tire tracks.

Elise fell on her butt in the mud, rose and continued her descent into the darkness, shaking the slick, cold slop from her hands and holding the flashlight as steady as possible. She shone the light back and forth, hoping to catch a glimpse of Luke.

When she reached the bottom of the road near the banks of the river, her heart beat an erratic pace, and she began to think maybe the killer had set a trap for her or her son. Frantic now, she whirled, her light barely penetrating the rain that had picked up since she'd left her house. A black SUV stood beside the river, the interior dark and menacing. Elise shone her light into the interior, but nothing moved. Luke was nowhere to be seen.

The river flowed heavily, swollen from the rain to ten feet deeper than usual. The dull roar of water rushing past masked most noises.

A faint cry carried over the top of the vehicle, over the noise of the river. Elise spun toward the bridge. Had the cry come from there? Elise shone the flashlight beam toward the underpinnings of the bridge. At first, she could see nothing but dark shadows and rain. Then the shadows moved and a man holding a small figure emerged

"Luke!" Elise ran toward them, her light bouncing across the gravel and brush, flashing on and off the man and boy. "Luke!" She called out, tears streaming from her eyes, washed away by the drenching rain.

"That's far enough," the man yelled.

Elise halted, holding her flashlight on the man and boy.

He had something pointed at Luke's head.

Her stomach tumbled over and over as she realized what it was. Oh, God, he had a gun pointed at her son's head and it wasn't Stan. It wasn't even a man she recognized. Yes, he had brown hair and dark eyes like her former husband, but it wasn't Stan. Elise wasn't sure if she should be relieved or not.

He'd already killed two women, and he held her son at gunpoint. But knowing it wasn't Stan had a strange impact on her. Almost relief, if she could have allowed herself the luxury of relief in such dire circumstances.

"Mama!" Luke reached out his arms.

Elise stumbled and fell to her knees. "Please, don't hurt him." Her chest tightened, her breath catching in her throat on a silent sob. "Please. You want me, not him."

"You got that right."

"Let him go. I'll go with you. I won't even put up a fight."

"Very convenient. The other ladies didn't put up a fight either. They thought they were with someone safe." When Luke wiggled to get out of his arms, he shook the boy. "Be still!"

"Let him go!" Elise staggered to her feet and ran forward.

Luke kicked out, landing a foot in the man's privates.

He threw Luke to the side and doubled over, his hand coming up to aim the gun at Elise. "Don't come any closer."

Luke lay on the concrete beneath the bridge, his body limp, unmoving.

"What have you done to my son, you monster?"

she growled through gritted teeth, anger overcoming her fear.

He grunted and halfway straightened, the barrel of the gun level with her chest. "Not nearly what I plan to do to you."

"Why? Why are you doing this to me? I don't even know you."

"Yeah, but somehow, you and your family have managed to kill my career. I feel like I should return the favor."

* * *

PAUL DIDN'T WAIT for Alvarez to get back with him on the GPS location of Cain's cell phone. "Get in the truck, Mel."

"Where are we going? We don't know where Cain took her until we hear back from Alvarez." Despite her arguments, she left Elise's house on Paul's heels and climbed into the truck beside him.

"He killed the other two women out by the river."

"Yeah, in two different locations. Each up different highways. If you take the wrong route, you could double our time getting back to the right one."

"I can't wait while he's got her." Paul's throat tightened. "He'll kill her."

"Do you think it's all because of a promotion he didn't get?"

Paul gave a brief nod.

Mel shook her head. "Unbelievable."

"I should have had him transferred as soon as I came in. None of this would have happened if I'd dealt with the problem instead of ignoring it." Paul slammed his palm against the steering wheel. "It's all my fault."

Mel gripped the handle above the door when the truck swerved. "You didn't know he'd go psycho. You couldn't have guessed he'd do what he's doing."

"I should have." He should have seen the signs much earlier. "Two women died, Mel. Because of me."

"Paul, you're not a mind reader. You can't go around believing the worst in everyone. Cain was supposed to be on our side—one of the good guys."

"I should have seen it. Then at least two innocent women wouldn't have become victims. Maybe even three." His throat closed off on the last word. He couldn't let Elise be the third victim. Whatever it took, he had to get there in time to stop Cain.

"If you believed the worst in people, you'd never have fallen in love with Elise."

"Who said I'm in love with Elise?" Although he tossed the words at Mel, he couldn't deny it. What he felt was stronger than any emotion he'd ever experienced with any other woman. If she died, he'd never get the chance to follow through and explore the possibilities of a happily-ever-after with her.

Mel snorted, rolling her eyes his way. "You are in

love with her, so don't try to scam me. A woman can tell."

His stomach knotted. How had he let this happen? How had he fallen in love with her when he'd only known her a few days? And how hopeless was loving Elise? "She doesn't want another man in her life. Stan really did a number on her."

"Yeah, but if I'm not mistaken, she's falling in love with you, too." Mel stared across the interior of the truck at him, her eyes shining in the light from the dashboard. "Given time, you two can work past the killer-ex thing."

Paul whipped out of the driveway onto the road. "None of it matters if Cain kills her."

"Then let's find her." Mel stared out the window. "You know she might have tried to call you on your cell phone. Have you checked your messages remotely?"

"Call my cell phone number." He gave her the instructions to access his messages, tapping his fingers on the steering wheel as he waited in the middle of the road.

"Here. Your messages are coming up. You have two." Mel shoved the phone against his ear.

"Paul! Luke is missing." Elise's panicked voice filled his ear. "I can't wait for you, I have to find him. I'm sorry I'm breaking my promise to stay put, but I have to go home."

Paul's jaw tightened at the fear in Elise's voice. He quickly skipped to the next message.

"Agent Fletcher, sir. This is Brandon Johnson." The boy sniffed into the phone. "Please come help my mom. We're at the Guadalupe River bridge on Highway 474. Please hurry."

Paul dropped the phone into Mel's lap and swung the truck in the direction of Highway 474 leading north out of Breuer.

"Who was it?" Mel asked.

"Brandon Johnson." A scared little boy who might not live to see the next day. And if he did, he might not have a mother or little brother to go home to.

"You know where they are, don't you." Mel held onto the handle above her door, her expression grim.

"Yes." He told her what he'd heard. "Ten minutes. It takes ten minutes to get there."

"Make it five." Melissa grabbed the handle above the door and held on.

Paul held the steering wheel so tightly his knuckles turned white. They had to get there in time. Elise needed him and he wouldn't let her down. Not again.

CHAPTER 17

"Please, take me. Don't hurt my son." Elise begged on her knees in the mud. She'd say anything, *do* anything to keep her son safe.

As she pushed against the ground to rise to her feet, her hand closed around a stone the size of a baseball. She curled her fingers around it and hid it behind her back, hoping her aim was as good as it had been when she'd played softball in high school. She'd have to be good. The rock and her brain were her only weapons in the face of certain death.

"What you don't understand, *Alice*, is that I'm in charge here. You don't get a say in what happens."

"My name is Elise." Anger washed over Elise's fear, pushing it aside to make room for more rage. "Who are you, anyway?"

"Your boyfriend doesn't talk about me? He never mentioned Trevor Cain?" He snorted. "Figures."

"What boyfriend? I've never heard of you, and I don't have a boyfriend."

"The man you slept with last night. Don't play dumb with me. I know what's going on." He kicked at the boy lying on the ground. "You and these brats are all he cares about."

"Did Paul have you sent to prison or something?"

The man laughed. "Hardly. I'm one of the good guys. I put the bad guys behind bars. Besides, he's not smart enough to figure out who's responsible for the deaths of those women. And I'm not going to give him the opportunity to figure it out. Helps when you don't leave any witnesses."

Elise's body went cold. She gulped hard to keep from screaming. She'd suspected as much. This man wouldn't be telling her as much as he was if he planned on letting her go. That went for Luke as well, which made it all the more imperative that she keep a level head and figure a way out of this on her own. "Paul's smarter than you are. At least he doesn't have to go around killing innocent women to prove he's a man."

The man's mouth tightened until his jaw twitched. "Fletcher hasn't got anything on me, except pure dumb luck. He couldn't even figure out this case before two women died. Make that three." He nodded at the gun in his hand. "Now, not only will he lose his golden-boy prestige, but he'll also lose the woman he's gotten stupid over. Seems like a fair trade to me. My career for his girlfriend. I'll bet you even helped him solve the Dakota Strangler case. What, were you and him doing it on the side while your husband killed those women?"

Anger flared inside her over his callous words. As Paul had said, *Stan* was responsible for the murders in North Dakota, not her. And just like Stan, *this* man was responsible for the deaths of Lauren and Mary. She couldn't let her emotions take over. She had to use her head. How ironic, when her husband hadn't wanted her to be smart or think for herself. Now she *had* to...or die.

She sucked in a deep, calming breath. "I don't know what you're talking about. None of this is making any sense." She inched closer, her worry for Luke outweighing her concern over the gun pointed at her chest. In order for the rock in her hand to be of any use, she had to get close enough to hit her mark. "What is your career, anyway? Murdering women?" Keep him talking, maybe she'd figure out some way to disarm him and get Luke away. Far away.

"No, murdering women was only my way of showing the world Mr. Perfect Agent Fletcher isn't so great after all. While he was out playing with you, women were dying, and he could do nothing to stop it."

"Paul will stop you." If she didn't stop him first.

"Sorry, but he won't. And he won't be able to save you or your son in time. Now won't that just kill him?" His laughter echoed off the concrete and steel of the underside of the bridge. "And the beauty of it all is that once you're gone, he'll lose his job and I'll be promoted in his place. With no one the wiser. The country will think the Dakota Strangler is still alive and killing."

Her heartbeat faltered. She knew Cain was a murderer but hearing him promise to kill her and her son made it all the more frightening. What he might not fully appreciate was that she wasn't going to die yet, nor was Luke, and she refused to go down without a helluva fight.

While he'd been talking, bragging about his prowess as a crafty murderer, Elise had worked her way closer until she stood within range to do some damage with her rock, *if* her aim struck true. *Please, please, please remember everything Coach Wright taught you about throwing a ball in high school.*

One shot was all she'd get.

"It's time." Cain turned his gun on Luke. "Should I start with him or you?"

Her arm tensed. As she drew it from behind her back, a flurry of motion burst into her peripheral vision. Before she could react, a small, dark shadow slammed into the man's arm, knocking the gun loose. It flew across the sloping concrete, skittering to a stop three feet short of the rising river water.

Oh, God. It was Brandon. Elise held her breath as her son scurried across the concrete to stand in front of Luke, his face fierce and scared at the same time.

"You little brat!" Cain dove for the gun.

"Duck, Brandon!" Elise cocked her arm, prayed for a miracle and let loose. Throwing into a stationary catcher's glove was a lot easier than at a moving target. But her rock hit Cain in the head, stopping him short of his gun. He stumbled and fell, rolling over and over until he tumbled into the water. The current picked him up and carried him downstream, past the bridge and out of sight of the flashlight Elise held.

Brandon ran for the gun and kicked it into the dark, muddy water roaring past.

"Run, Brandon!" Elise scooped Luke up in her arms. His little body wiggled against hers, filling her with relief. "Hold still, little guy. We'll get you home."

Uncertain whether Cain had been revived by the cold river water, Elise knew she had to get to her car as quickly as possible.

Brandon stumbled behind her, slipping in the muddy ruts left by Cain's truck.

Weighed down by Luke, Elise slowed and turned, extending the hand holding the flashlight for him. "Grab the flashlight and hold on."

Brandon latched onto the light and pulled himself up next to her. Then he let go and charged forward. "Come on!"

Getting to the top of the hill seemed to take

forever. Elise slipped at least another five times, crashing to the ground on her elbows. She rolled to the side to keep from crushing Luke. Brandon had disappeared, hopefully making it to the car and the cell phone to call for help.

Luke wiggled to get free. "Let go, Mom. I can walk."

Unable to push herself back to her feet without letting go, Elise released him.

Once free, Luke stood in the mud, slipped and scrambled to his feet, running after Brandon.

With rain dripping down in her eyes, and mud coating her arms and legs, Elise struggled to get up.

Before she could take a step, the ground shook behind her and a large hand grabbed her ankle.

Barely balanced to begin with, Elise crashed to the drenched earth, the wind knocked from her lungs. But she held onto the flashlight, its heavy batteries making it the only weapon she had left to save herself and her boys. "Run, Luke! Run, Brandon! Hide!"

Fingers grabbed the back of her calf and Trevor Cain crawled up her body, one hand at a time.

Trapped on her stomach, Elise rolled from side to side, unable to flip onto her back. She swung the flashlight out to the side.

His grunt told her she'd made contact, but not enough to get him off her back.

Again, she swung the heavy flashlight.

He let go of one of her legs long enough to grab the flashlight and yank it from her grip, tossing it into the bushes, the light shining off in another direction.

Now, it was her against him. Darkness swallowed them, rain pelting her face and running into her eyes. She kicked, she rolled, but he was heavy, and the mud made it too slippery for her to gain purchase. Elise needed a miracle about now to save her and her boys.

Cain climbed onto her back, straddling her hips with his. He yanked a handful of her hair, pulling back hard until she thought her neck would snap.

"I should have killed you first." He slammed her face into the mud.

If the ground hadn't been so soft and moist, the force of his brutal slam would surely have broken her nose. As it was, her mouth and nostrils filled with mud, choking off her air.

He lifted her head again for another slam.

Elise spit and blew the mud from her nose, gasping for breath. Was this the way it would end? She prayed Luke and Brandon were far, far away and hiding low in the bushes. She prayed it would all end very quickly and painlessly.

"Say goodbye to your boys. They're next." His hand tightened on her hair and his body tensed for the next slam.

Then Cain jerked off her back and fell across her legs, sliding down the muddy slope.

Stunned, Elise kicked free of Cain's legs and rolled to the side, scuttling to her feet to bump into a broad, solid chest.

"Paul!" She fell into his arms, her body sliding against his, coating him in a layer of mud.

* * *

PAUL CLUTCHED HER TO HIM, regardless of the mud. Feeling her soft body against his helped to slow his heartbeat and steady his breathing. He'd never been more scared in his life than when he'd seen Cain brutalizing her. Now, he didn't want to let go of her. Ever again.

"Stay with Elise. I want to take care of this." Melissa pushed around Paul's side, gun drawn, and stalked down the hill toward the man who'd terrorized Breuer for the past week.

"Don't kill him, Melissa," Paul called out. Much as he wanted to see the man die for all he'd done, Paul knew he had to live by the laws he'd sworn to uphold. "The families of the victims will want justice."

"I'll show him justice." In the limited glow from the fallen flashlight, Melissa stopped in front of Cain. "Come on, coward. Your murdering days are done."

"What's wrong, Fletcher," Cain called out from flat on his back in the mud. "Not man enough to take me on? Have to send a *woman* to do your job? Took you long enough to figure it out. So much for being a hero."

"Cuff him and read him his rights, Mel." Paul's arm tightened around Elise. He pushed a muddy strand of hair from her face. "Are you okay?"

Elise nodded and snuggled into his chest.

Paul couldn't tell if it was tears or more rain that soaked his shirt.

She looked up at him, her face filthy but the most beautiful face he'd ever seen. "Luke and Brandon?"

"Safe in my truck, although I think they're pretty scared." He returned his attention to Cain. "You should join them." Although he said the words, he didn't loosen his grip on her.

Melissa bent toward Cain, handcuffs outstretched. "Take a swing, try something. I'd love to get one in for the women you terrorized and murdered."

"Don't, Mel," Paul said. "He's not worth it. He's nothing but a coward. He didn't get the job I did, not because of me, but because he couldn't handle it."

"Don't ignore me, Fletcher. You'll never be the agent I am. You're just not that good. You didn't deserve that promotion. I did!" The man on the muddy ground, surged to his feet with a roar and shoved at Mel hard.

Caught off guard, she slipped and fell in the mud, cursing her own stupidity.

But before Cain could reach Paul, Melissa flung

out her leg, catching the killer in the shins, bringing him to his knees. Then she was on his back, slamming his body into the ground, her arm around his throat, pulling hard until he gasped for air.

"Like the way that feels?" she said, her voice low and angry. "Like being helpless and scared? You ought to try it sometime. I'm sure the guys in the prison you're going to will love practicing on you. They eat agents for lunch."

"Mel." Paul set Elise to the side and went to Cain. "He's not worth it."

For a moment she hesitated, her eyes blazing. Then she loosened her hold on Cain's throat and stood, bringing one of his arms up hard between his shoulder blades, keeping the man immobile, his cheek in the mud.

Paul retrieved a plastic zip-tie out of his pocket and cinched the man's hands together behind him, then yanked him to his feet. "It's over, Cain. The killing, your career...it's over."

Sirens penetrated the roar of the river and the drenching rain. Flashing lights pierced the darkness as several police cars skidded to a stop on the road above them.

Paul's gaze scanned the dimly lit path leading up to Elise's car. She'd disappeared. Probably headed for her boys. Which was just as well. He had a lot to explain to the police and his boss at the Bureau before he could check on her, Luke and Brandon.

Though the murders had been solved, and Elise and her boys were alive, Paul couldn't help his confusion. Now that Trevor had confessed to the killings, would Elise still want to stay in Breuer?

Paul hoped she'd stay. The last time he'd been with her in North Dakota, the timing hadn't been right. He couldn't consider this encounter as good timing either. But if he'd learned one thing out of all of this mess, he couldn't wait for perfect timing. He had to reach out for what he wanted and hope she wanted it, too.

"Let's go, Cain. I'm ready for this night to be over." He hauled the killer up the mud-slick road to the highway above, delivering him into the hands of Sheriff Engel.

An ambulance stood to the side, the back door open, Elise climbing in to join Brandon and Luke. More than anything, Paul wanted to go with them to make sure the boys and their mother were all right. Luke sported a nasty bruise on his forehead when Paul had run across him and Brandon standing on the highway, crying and scared for their mother.

A fresh wave of anger washed over him. He thought he'd lost Elise. Seeing her face down in the mud with Cain beating the crap out of her had nearly driven him over the edge. He'd kicked the man so hard, he wouldn't be surprised if he'd cracked a few of Cain's ribs.

The ambulance drove away as Paul answered

questions for the sheriff. He'd catch up with them at the hospital. They'd need a ride home.

When the sheriff took off in the squad car with Trevor Cain, Paul headed for his truck.

Melissa ducked into the driver's side of Elise's car. "Keys are here. I'll take her car back by her house to pick up my truck. You're going to the hospital, right?" Melissa grinned at Paul.

"Yeah. Thanks." Now that he was free for the moment, he wondered if Elise would care to see him anymore. Had their one night of passion been a fluke? Adrenaline sex for tough times? Would she want anything to do with him after all that had happened?

Paul wouldn't be surprised if she wanted to forget all about North Dakota and Breuer. Heck, she'd probably want to pack up and leave as soon as she could. Start over once again.

His jaw tightened as he pulled out on the highway. Somehow, he had to convince her that she didn't have to leave. That she could start over right here in Breuer. Maybe give their relationship more than a fighting chance. One thing was certain—he needed help.

CHAPTER 18

ELISE SAT beside Brandon in the waiting room of the emergency room at Santa Rosa Children's Hospital in San Antonio. Luke had a cold compress on his forehead and was sleeping, stretched across Elise's lap. The doctor told her to wake him several times during the night in case of concussion, but that he should be all right.

Agent Melissa Bradley had called to tell her that someone would be there in a few minutes to take her home. She wouldn't have to come into the police station to answer questions until tomorrow, when Trevor Cain was securely locked up in jail.

As she sat with one arm around Brandon and the other cradling Luke, she wondered if it was time to move on.

As if on cue, her cell phone rang. Hoping it would be Paul, she answered, her voice breathless. "Hello."

"Alice!" Her sister's voice shouted in her ear. "I just heard. Oh, my God, I can't believe all this happened to you. I'm taking a leave of absence and getting on a plane in the morning. I would have been out tonight, but they've got some wind advisories keeping all planes from entering or leaving Minneapolis tonight."

"It's okay, Brenna. I'm fine, the boys are fine. It's all over."

"When I got the call from Fletcher, I couldn't believe it. I should have been there with you."

"Really, I'm okay." Elise smiled, for what seemed the first time in a week. "You don't need to come down here. You have to think of yourself and your baby. Flying at eight months pregnant probably isn't a good idea. I'm sure you'd make the flight attendants nervous. Besides, they caught the guy."

"That's what I heard. I can't believe it was another agent." Her sister sighed. "Are you sure you're okay? I'd feel better seeing you in person."

Elise thought of the bruise on her cheek and Luke's forehead and shook her head. The outward wounds would heal quickly. Getting Brandon and Luke over the trauma of the kidnapping might take a little longer. But they'd muddle through together. "No. We'll be okay."

"If you're sure..."

"I'm sure."

"I tried to call you earlier, but my cell phone

reception stunk. I wanted to tell you that I'd spent the day on the phone with a number of agencies and hospitals located along the Red River south of Riverton."

Elise's heart rate kicked up a notch. Although they'd captured the Breuer killer, they still didn't have a definitive answer about her husband. For all she knew, he could still be out there, waiting for his chance to make her life hell. "Did they find anything?"

"Hospitals came up blank. But I found a small town along the river who'd recovered a John Doe skeleton just recently. They'd done a dental X-ray but couldn't find a match locally. I had the North Dakota crime lab run a comparison against Stan's dental records and guess what?"

Elise's eyes filled with tears and her hand shook. "It matched?" she whispered, afraid voicing her heartfelt hopes, would jinx her yet again.

"It matched, sweetie. Stan Klaus is well and truly dead. You don't have to run anymore."

With her eyes blurred by tears, Elise didn't see the group of people walking in the door. Brandon jumped up from his seat beside her, shouting, "Kenny! Alex!"

Elise brushed the moisture from her eyes and cheeks and looked up at a group of people walking toward her in the emergency room lobby. Principal Ford, Kendall and Alex.

"What's going on?" Brenna asked in Elise's ear.

"I have to go. I'll call you back later." Brenna kept talking, but Elise hit the off button and stood, hugging Luke's sleeping body next to her. Had word gotten out? Had she been exposed for the serial killer's wife? Was her entire world about to crash around her?

Principal Ford stepped forward. "Ms. Johnson...Elise." She held out her arms and engulfed Elise in a giant hug, taking in Luke and her in the effort. Kendall and Alex crowded in, all trying to hug her, everyone talking at once.

The one face she didn't see was Paul's. When Melissa said someone would be there to pick her up, she'd thought it would be Paul. Throughout the outpouring of well-wishes, hugs and love, Elise tried to hide her disappointment.

Kendall nudged Principal Ford. "Are you going to tell her?"

The principal smiled and winked at Kendall and Alex. "No, I think you two should."

Kendall cleared her throat. "Ms. Johnson, we just wanted to let you know how much of a difference you've made in our lives."

Elise wanted to laugh, but tears choked her throat from making any noises. Those tears flowed down her cheeks now.

"Yeah, and we know about what happened to you up in North Dakota," Alex said.

Lead dropped to the pit of Elise's gut, followed by overwhelming sadness. She'd have to leave. To uproot the boys once again and leave.

Kendall pulled Brandon under one arm, hugging him. "We know about the Dakota Strangler and what you, Brandon and Luke have lived through since then."

Yeah, her days in Breuer were definitely numbered. She stared at Kendall, Alex and Principal Ford. She'd miss them. Had it been too much to hope she could find a home for herself and her boys? Were they destined to move from town to town for the rest of their lives? "Does everyone know?"

"Yeah, pretty much." Kendall nodded. "The news reporters got a hold of it and aired it when they captured Agent Cain."

"When Agent Fletcher put the call out to me and Kendall, we knew we had to do something to convince you."

"Agent Fletcher?" Through the darkness of her depressing thoughts, a light of hope burned like a reviving ember buried deep in the ashes.

"Yes, Agent Fletcher." His deep voice rumbled from the lobby entrance, and the students and principal parted, letting him come through to the front.

Paul stood with a cowboy hat in his hands, his shirt muddy from when she'd clung to him out by the river and his face streaked with grime. But he was the most beautiful man she'd ever seen. She stood, holding Luke in her arms, afraid to move, afraid to say anything to douse the tiny flickers of optimism daring to build inside.

"As soon as I heard the radio make a big announcement about the capture of the copycat Dakota Strangler, I knew you'd be thinking about leaving." Paul's brows rose, challenging her to deny it.

She couldn't. Even now, everyone in Breuer would know she'd been married to a killer. Leaving would be her only choice.

"Mom, I don't want to leave," Brandon said, looking up to Kendall and Alex. "I have friends here."

"I know, honey. I know." She hugged Luke tighter.

He stirred, his eyes opening. Her youngest son blinked once, then again, focusing on the tall man in front of him. Then he held out his arms to Paul.

Paul lifted him and laid him on his shoulder. "How are you, big guy?" The small boy and the big man with the sandy blond hair and blue eyes, almost the color of hers looked right together.

For a fleeting moment, Elise wished Paul were a permanent part of her family. The father the boys deserved, the man she could possibly learn to love. "I can't stay. You, of all people, know why."

"You can't go. We need more teachers like you," Principal Ford insisted. "I suspected you had a history and that something wasn't quite right, but I also saw how much you wanted the job, how much you cared whether or not the students did well."

"Yeah, besides, we love you, Ms. Johnson." Kendall hugged Brandon. "And we love Brandon and Luke."

"Yeah," Alex said. "You can't leave us. What would the school do without you?"

Paul smiled over Luke's head. "Everyone wants you to stay in Breuer."

Suddenly shy and with nothing to hold in front of her, Elise felt exposed, raw, emotional. More tears pushed their way into her eyes and spilled down her cheeks. "Everyone?"

"Everyone." Paul reached out and brushed his thumb across her cheek. "Including me."

"Why? I don't know if we can be anything more than friends."

Paul's smile faded, his blue eyes serious. "Then I'll settle for that."

"You'd be my friend?" Elise's heart swelled at that. "Stan had never wanted to be my friend."

"I keep telling you, I'm not Stan." Paul laughed. "When are you going to start believing me?"

"He's really dead," she whispered.

Paul tucked a strand of hair behind her ear. "Yes, he is."

"Brenna told you?"

"News on the grapevine travels fast."

Elise couldn't stop the sob from rising up her throat. "I'm free."

Paul pulled her into his arms and held her, Luke crushed between them. Brandon broke away from

Kendall and pushed his way in between Elise and Paul, so they stood hugging, just like a family. "So, what's it going to be? Are you going to stay and give these folks a chance to know and love you?"

Elise nodded, for the first time in two years daring to hope. "On one condition."

"And that is?" Paul kissed the tip of her nose.

"I get to know you as well." She leaned up on her toes and pressed her lips to his.

"Good, because I still have a fence to build and a puppy to get settled. I promised the boys." Then he kissed her long and hard and a cheer went up from the crowd. When he came up for air, he smiled and held her close. "Then it's settled. You're coming home."

She nestled into his chest, her arms around him and her boys. The promise of a bright future ahead, with the chance to get to know this tall, handsome man filled her with a happiness she never dreamed would come her way. "I'm coming home."

EPILOGUE

Five months later...

"Fetch!" Luke called out as he threw the tennis ball for the fifteenth time.

Titan, the four-month-old sable German Shepherd mix, dashed across the backyard. Still a puppy with gangly legs, he skidded to a stop seconds before crashing into the back fence. He made a clumsy leap into the air, caught the ball between his teeth, and trotted back toward the boy, his tail swishing side to side.

Luke took the ball from Titan and handed it to George, the high school janitor and Luke's friend. "Here, George, you throw it this time."

Elise's heart warmed at the man's smile as he took his turn, throwing the ball for Titan.

Paul, Elise and the boys had spent a weekend clearing the brush off the back of the property between Elise's house and George's. When they'd built the fence, Paul had installed a gate between the two yards, making it easier for George and Luke to visit with strict rules on keeping it closed so the puppies couldn't get out.

On the porch, Athena, the surprise puppy that had chosen Brandon, lay sprawled across the wooden deck, leaning against Brandon, having tired of playing chase, content to roll onto her back for the belly rubs Brandon provided every time she was near.

After they'd finished building the fence, Paul had loaded them all into his truck, took them to the local shelter where he'd heard they'd just received a litter of puppies that had been left on their doorstep in a cardboard box. They'd arrived to find nine wiggling pups, eager to find new homes. The staff had allowed the boys to enter the pen and play with the puppies.

Luke had chosen the pup wrestling with his brothers and sisters and then came up to him and licked him on the cheek.

Brandon had sat close to the squirming mass of pups. All but one of them came up to sniff him and crawl across his lap. The last one, a solid black female, stood away from the others, smaller, scared and looking a little sad.

Paul had leaned down to Brandon and told him that solid black pups were sometimes the last to be adopted.

Brandon's brow had furrowed, his gaze on the black female.

Once the others moved back to Luke, the black one came up to Brandon, crawled into his lap and fell asleep. He couldn't leave her behind.

They'd gone into the shelter for one puppy and came home with two. Though Elise hadn't wanted the puppies to sleep with the boys, they'd ended up in their beds every night and seemed to help soothe them when they had nightmares.

Elise stood beside Mel at the grill Paul had insisted on purchasing, saying *a backyard wasn't complete without one*.

Mel flipped a couple of hamburgers, removed all the hotdogs from the top rack and placed them on the platter Elise held out. She tipped her chin toward Brandon and Luke. "How are they doing?"

"Luke isn't as eager to run out of the house without permission, though I expect he'll be back to his old antics soon." Elise sighed as she glanced toward her older son. "Brandon still has nightmares and is super protective of his little brother and me. Having Paul here most evenings and on the weekends, teaching the boys how to use a hammer and build things has made them feel safer."

"The entire community of Bruer feels safer with Cain locked up," Mel said.

A shiver of horror rippled down Elise's spine at the mention of the monster who'd come so close to killing her sons. Her gaze went to her children, who'd been through more than any child should have to endure. "I'm glad he won't get out on bail."

Mel lowered her voice, her gaze going to Brandon on the porch. "No way Cain's ever getting out of jail with two counts of murder and three counts of attempted murder."

"Good," Elise said, her lips pressing together. "He should have to rot there for what he did to those two women."

"I can't get over the weather here in March," Mel said.

"Right? Back in North Dakota, they still have snow on the ground." Elise smiled. "I like that the boys can play outside more here."

"How's your sister holding up as a new mother?"

"Better," Elise said with a grin. "Grace is finally sleeping through the night."

"Are they coming for the wedding?" Mel asked.

Elise's brow furrowed. "Wedding?"

Mel blinked. "You mean Paul hasn't popped the question yet?" She snorted. "He practically lives here. He might as well make it official."

"Oh, you must be mistaken." Her cheeks heating,

Elise shrugged and looked away. "I think Paul feels responsible for what happened, but I told him it wasn't his fault. Just like he told me, it wasn't my fault that my husband was a serial killer. He's been such a good friend and so helpful with the boys."

"Friend, huh?" Mel shook her head. "Speak of the devil, where is he?" Mel held up her spatula. "He's supposed to be manning the grill."

"He called an hour ago and said he'd be late. He was held up at the office."

Mel frowned. "On a Saturday? He didn't say anything to me about it."

"He didn't want you to worry. He should be here soon."

"Are those burgers I smell?" Paul's voice boomed from the side of the house where he'd installed the second gate, making it wide enough to drive a truck or a riding lawnmower through.

When he emerged, Elise's heart soared. He had that effect on her and it never got old. She'd fallen in love with this man who was kind, gentle, brave and good. And her boys were blossoming into kind, helpful young men just by following his example. He'd be a good father.

Her heart fluttered and she pressed a hand to her chest. Since the one time they'd made love, he hadn't done more than kiss her. After all that had happened, he probably didn't feel the same.

Paul was followed by another woman with black hair pulled straight back from her forehead and light-colored eyes. She wore tailored black slacks and a white button-down shirt open at the collar. Despite her austere clothing, she was a striking woman.

A sad stab of envy touched Elise to the core. Had Paul cooled on her because of this woman? Elise could understand why.

"I meant to be here earlier, but I had something come up. Namely, our newest team member, arriving a couple days early. I'd like you to meet the newest member of our team, Avery Hart. She transferred in from the Memphis office."

Mel and Elise hurried forward to shake Avery's hand, welcoming her to the team of FBI agents in the San Antonio office.

Luke and George continued playing with the ball and Titan.

Elise took the spatula from Mel's hand. "I'll take over. I'm sure you three have things to discuss."

She returned to the grill and removed the burgers, placing them beside the hotdogs while Mel, Paul and Avery exchanged introductions.

Brandon came down the porch steps and held out his hand like a little man and said, "Nice to meet you." His manners made Elise proud and sad at the same time. Stan had hammered good manners into Brandon, cutting him no slack whatsoever.

Athena chose that moment to rejoin the fun in the yard. Brandon followed.

"At the same time Avery showed up, we got a call from Tyler, Texas, with a request for help with two murders. The sheriff's afraid it could be the beginning of a serial killer case. He wants all the help he can get before he loses another victim in his county. Avery is heading up there tomorrow after we get her entered into our system."

Elise gave Avery half a smile, feeling suddenly inadequate. As a schoolteacher, how could she compete with a tough-as-nails FBI agent? A schoolteacher with two small children. Not that there was any competition. Paul had been at her house almost every day since they'd closed the Breuer Murders Case. Why hadn't he made a move on her? Elise had no idea what his intentions were toward her.

"Now that you've met Avery, I can't wait any longer."

Elise turned with the tray of burgers and hotdogs. "The burgers are done. We can eat now, if you're that hungry."

He took the tray from Elise and handed it to Mel. Then he took both of Elise's hands and called out, "Brandon, Luke, initiate big surprise."

Brandon blinked. "Now?"

Paul nodded. "Now."

Elise tugged on her hands, but Paul held steady but gently. "Hang on a minute. The boys have a mission they've trained for." He lifted his chin toward Elise's sons.

Luke and Brandon ran to the doghouse they'd helped build that the dogs had yet to use and dove inside. After a scuffling around, they emerged. Brandon was out first, carrying what looked like small white pieces of posterboard close to their chests, mischievous smiles fluttering across their lips.

A few feet from where Paul held Elise's hands, they stopped.

"Ready?" Paul asked.

"Ready, sir," Brandon responded.

Paul nodded. "Proceed with Operation Big Leap."

"What's this all about?" Elise asked, her pulse pounding through her veins.

"Shh," Paul hushed her. "Let them proceed."

Elise clamped her lips closed and watched as Brandon flipped a white sheet of posterboard over. On it were written bold letters drawn with marker pens.

MOM

Brandon laid his board on the ground and stood back.

Luke struggled and almost dropped his stack of boards. Finally, he flipped one that was drawn in crayon.

WILL YOU

Luke laid his first card on the ground and straightened.

Brandon held up his next card.

MARRY

Elise's heart leaped into her throat. She pressed a hand to her mouth, holding her breath as Luke struggled with his cards and dropped one on the ground.

PAUL

Brandon's lips twisted and a frown settled across his forehead. He laid out the remainder of his cards on the ground.

The words didn't make sense.

SO CAN YOUR AND DAD?

Brandon grabbed Luke's set and tried to take them from him.

"No," Luke said. "These are mine. I'll do it." He dropped the cards face-up on the ground.

HE BE HUSBAND OUR

Brandon quickly rearranged the words.

MOM WILL YOU MARRY PAUL SO HE CAN BE YOUR HUSBAND AND OUR DAD?

Elise's eyes welled with tears at the message.

"Please?" Luke clasped his hands together. "We like him a lot. The dogs love him too."

Movement out of the corner of her eye made her turn back toward Paul.

The man had dropped to his knee

Elise gasped and stared down at a red velvet box in his hand.

"Dearest Elise, I thought I could keep my distance from you and let you have all the time you needed to recover from past events, but I couldn't wait another minute to let you know how I feel." He opened the box to display a beautiful marquis diamond. "I know it's too soon for you to make a decision, but I wanted you to know how I have always felt about you. I love you."

"But I come with—"

"Two little men who are the strongest, bravest and most protective guys I've ever known."

Brandon and Luke stood taller, their chins rising.

Elise wanted to laugh and cry at the same time.

"I love them as much as I love you. They're a part of you and I'd be honored to be a part of your family."

A lump lodged in Elise's throat, blocking any words she might say. A single tear escaped an eye and slid down her cheek.

Paul reached out with his free hand and brushed away the tear. "I know this is too soon, but I'm putting it out there," he said softly.

Elise shook her head. "I was married to a serial killer."

"That fact does not define you," Paul said. "If you choose to reject my proposal, I'll understand, but at least I will have tried. Think about it and take all the time you need. In the meantime, I won't spoil the rest of the party." Paul closed the box and started to rise.

Before he could, Elise dropped to her knees and took his hands, box and all in hers. "Wait. I've thought about it. You're so good with the boys. They need a father to set a good example for them."

"You'd marry me just for your boys?" Paul shook his head. "I'd do it, just to be in your life. But I love all three of you."

"No, that's not the only reason," She held tightly to his hands, afraid to let him walk away. "I didn't trust my judgment after Stan. I thought what we had was a good enough marriage. But I know better now. Because of you." She lifted his hands to press her lips to his knuckles. "You taught me friendship is as important as sexual attraction and that couples could work together as partners, not one controlling the other. You're the father my boys deserve. I don't need time to think. I know what I want."

"Then say it already," Mel said. "The suspense is killing us."

"I love you, Paul Fletcher. I'll marry you as long as Brandon and Luke agree."

Paul's eyes brightened. "Boys, what do you say to all three of us getting married and letting me adopt you as my sons?"

Brandon let out the first happy yelp Elise had ever heard from him and rushed forward with Luke on his heels. They launched themselves at Elise and Paul, knocking them to the ground, laughing and hugging.

Titan and Athena joined them in the happiest dogpile Elise could have ever loved.

Her nightmare life had come to an end and a new

life stretched before her full of friendship, adventure and love.

She hugged her family, dogs and all and laughed her joy aloud.

~ * ~

Thank you for reading SCORCHED. The next exciting book in A Killer Series is ERASED. Click HERE to preorder now.

RAVEN'S WATCH

RAVEN'S CLIFF BOOK #1

New York Times & *USA Today*
Bestselling Author

ELLE JAMES
&
KRIS NORRIS

RAVEN'S CLIFF

RAVEN'S WATCH

NY TIMES BEST SELLING AUTHOR

ELLE JAMES
KRIS NORRIS

PROLOGUE

JSOC MISSION... Undisclosed location

"Beckett."

Major Foster Beckett nodded at his copilot, Sean Hansen, before banking the helicopter over as the next burst of machine gun fire whizzed past the chopper, lighting up the darkness behind them. "I know, buddy. This guy just won't give up."

He tipped the machine farther forward, picking up speed as he skimmed across the top of a ridge then dropped the bird down the other side. Barely missing a crumbling wall as it materialized out of the night.

One of his four teammates groaned in the rear cabin. Whether it was from the way Foster tossed the helicopter around or because they were on the verge of bleeding out, he wasn't sure. But if he didn't lose the bogey on his tail, it wouldn't matter.

They'd all be dead.

Sean made a wet, gurgling sound, and Foster nearly plowed the machine into the ground as he snapped his attention toward his buddy, wondering how it had all gone sideways so fast.

The damn spooks.

Once again, the CIA had screwed them over. Because Foster bet his ass the agency knew two of their agents were dirty. That they'd set up Foster and his crew as bait when their supposed rescue mission had turned into a shootout minutes into the return flight. Calm, cool extraction one moment, an all-out attack the next with Agent Stein and Agent Adams leading the charge. The one scenario his teammates hadn't counted on. Not when they'd been working with the bastards for the past six months. Men they thought could be trusted. Would have their backs. Discovering they were the ones selling intel…

Foster should have recognized the signs over the past few weeks. The beads of sweat along their brows. The slight twitch in their hands. Their increasing reluctance to look Foster or his buddies in the eyes.

And now, his brothers were paying the price.

He banked again, narrowly avoiding the next round of gunfire. "Hang in there, Sean. Once I lose this asshole, we'll be back on course."

Sean panted, lifting his arm and jabbing his finger at the only nav screen still working — leaving a bloody smear across the surface. "Here."

Foster frowned, dodging up and over another ridge before following the hill around to the right. Hugging the surface to the point dirt and stones kicked out behind him in twin eddies. "I realize we're desperate but even I think that's crazy."

Not that it stopped him from altering his course. Heading for that speck on the map glaring at him from beneath the smear of blood. Rain splattered across the bubble, flashes of lightning giving him fleeting glimpses of the landscape. A bulging rock face on his right. A lone tower on his left. What might be his saving grace when damn near every other navigational aid was dead. Even his night vision had gotten damaged, leaving him with nothing more than that one flickering nav screen and twenty years' worth of experience.

Foster hit the winding gulley leading to the narrow opening going as fast as the aircraft could handle. More than it could handle based on the how the controls vibrated in his grasp, the odd alarm chirping to life. He divided his attention between the screen and the walls quickly closing in on him, mentally counting down the distance.

He was about twenty feet back when he banked the chopper hard to the right, holding it steady as the sluggish controls fought to respond — definitely a hydraulic leak hampering the inputs.

The gap appeared in front of him like an abyss spiraling into the rock. The utter darkness drawing them in. He hit the tunnel going some insane speed, the controls still shaking as the engine whined from the strain. Any hint of light cut out. Even the nav blinked off for a few moments before he shot out the other side, a welcomed flash of lightning saving him from flying the machine into the side of the cliff as it curved around in front of them.

He cranked the helicopter over, trying to get more distance between them and the opening when the chopper surged forward as the sky lit up behind him, the force of the explosion spinning the aircraft.

Flames erupted from the fissure, parts of the other chopper whizzing through the air. Something hit the back end, pitching them sideways as a shrill whine echoed through the cabin. It took a few moments to get the bird stabilized, the controls like lead weights in his hands, with the last impact claiming what little hydraulics he'd had left.

Sean coughed, splattering blood across the window as he met Foster's gaze. "Hooyah."

"I got lucky. Nothing more."

Sean shook his head, his mouth pursing tight as he tapped his chest pocket. "My letter…"

Foster grunted, wishing he could move his arm enough to punch Sean in his thigh. "No. No talking about that damn death letter we've all written. You're going to be fine. You just have to push through."

"Beck…"

"I mean it Sean. Don't you dare give up…" He cursed under his breath, giving Sean a nod when his friend managed to reach out and leave a bloody handprint on his arm. "I'll get it to Cheryl. I promise."

Sean nodded, closing his eyes as a shudder raced down him, blood seeping through the bandages around his neck and ribs. He'd taken the brunt of the attack when Stein had opened fire, lunging over to cover Foster after Foster had gotten hit twice in the shoulder. Their pararescue medic and Foster's best friend, Chase Remington, had done what he could to minimize the bleeding once he and his other buddies had dealt with Adams and Stein, but it was obvious it wasn't working.

Foster huffed. "Stay with me, brother. I've got this baby turned around. I'll have you on the ground and into a surgical room within fifteen. Ten, if I can get more speed out of her."

Sean chuckled, the raspy sound fading into that eerie gurgling noise as his head lolled back and he slumped against the window.

"Sean! Damn it, Chase, I think he's coding."

Chase popped into view, his hands covered in blood. "I need a minute, Foster."

"Sean doesn't have a minute."

"Neither do Zain or Kash. I can only spread myself so thin."

"We're not dead yet, dumbass." Zain Everett — their SAR specialist, sniper and all 'round badass. Though it sounded as if he was even worse than Chase had hinted at. "Take care of Sean."

Chase pursed his lips, fisting his hands for a moment before vanishing then reappearing with an armful of supplies. He checked Sean's neck, looking back at Foster before applying more bandages and giving the guy a shot of something.

Chase turned to face him, mouth pinched tight. Eyes shadowed. Blood oozed from a gash on his forehead, more soaking the hem of his shirt. What looked like multiple hits to his vest.

Chase had been with Foster from the start. Had been the one constant throughout his career — until they'd met Sean, Rhett, Zain and Kash a dozen years ago. The six of them had fallen into sync on their very first mission, and they'd fought hard to stay together since.

Chase tugged on the tape holding Foster's shoulder together, muttering obscenities under his breath. "Your damn shoulder's a mess. I'm not sure how you're even moving that arm. Everything's shattered."

Foster would have shoved him off if he'd had the strength. Instead, he merely nodded toward Sean. "How is he?"

Chase glanced away, making it look as if he was getting more supplies out of his bag. "He's lost at least two liters of blood, and I'm out of saline and plasma."

"But if I get him back…"

"You just focus on staying conscious as long as possible. Try to get us as close as you can to the base. Okay?"

"Chase…"

"I'm just a medic, buddy. I can't raise the dead."

Foster looked over at Sean. He hadn't moved in the past few minutes, his skin so damn white he swore it was see-through. "No. It can't end like this. You have to do something. That should have been me. My blood. My sacrifice. He's got a wife. Kids. I have to…"

To what? Save him? Because Foster knew if Chase couldn't save Sean, no one could.

Chase packed more gauze around Foster's wounds, adding another layer of tape. "Let me check on the others, then I'll be back. Do what I can to help keep you awake."

"You worry about Zain, Kash and Rhett. I'll be okay."

"No, you won't." Chase cut him off. "You're bleeding through the clotting powder. Your face is nearly as white as Sean's and your good hand is shaking so bad, I'm surprised the damn chopper isn't vibrating through the air."

"My hand's shaking because I've lost hydraulics. Go. I'll shout if I'm gonna pass out."

"Right, because self-preservation has always been first on your list. Just, don't fucking die on me."

"Says the man who's bleeding worse than me. And yeah, I noticed. How bad are you hit?"

"Enough I'm extremely pissed."

Chase disappeared, Zain's groan sounding above the engines a moment later. The fact Foster hadn't heard their flight engineer, Rhett Oliver, utter so much as a sigh since his team had finally overpowered Stein and Adams meant the guy was either dead or unconscious. Just like their dog handler, Kash Sinclair.

The engine chugged, dropping the bird several feet before it stabilized. They couldn't afford to land. Not while they were fifty miles from safety with Foster's entire team struggling to hold on.

Which meant, milking every ounce of speed out of the aircraft. Taking it as close to the edge as possible without actually blowing the engines or killing the transmission. That fine line between all-out and too far. One he'd skirted on more occasions than he should be proud of. But the mission and his team always came first.

Not team. Family. That's what they were to him. Brothers. Men he'd kill for. Or die to protect. The only reason he'd made it through twenty years without losing his sanity.

His soul.

To think it would go down like this — betrayed by their own people. Lost on the wrong side of a volatile border. A fate he could alter if he rose to the challenge. Pushed past his limits.

Rain pummeled the bubble, the lone wiper barely keeping up. Not that he could see much with streaks of black cutting across his vision. But he kept that bird pointed north. Kept the machine on the verge of crapping out as he raced across the landscape, the wind and thunder following in his wake. Like Apollo chasing them with his chariot.

Was it getting colder? Darker? Or was Foster simply running out of time.

Chase's hand closed over his good shoulder, jerking him back from that numbing haze. "If you have to put her down..."

Foster shook his head, pounding the heel of his other hand against his temple in an effort to clear his vision. "Not... an option."

"Foster. Brother, you're barely holding on."

He shook his head again. Or maybe he'd only thought it. He couldn't tell. Could barely feel his fingers he was so cold. "How..."

Shit. One word. That's all he managed before his tongue got too heavy to form more.

"Don't worry about anyone else. That's my job. You focus on flying and not hitting the ground."

"Can't..."

Another one-word reply. And it cost him. Had more than just his good hand shaking. He wet his lips, forcing his eyelids open. Glancing over at Sean whenever he wanted to pack it in. Give up. Because if there was even a glimmer of hope he could still be saved…

Bile crested his throat, his eyes burning as he stared at the raging storm beyond the glass. The lightning hardly making a difference in his visibility, anymore. It was too late. He knew it. Felt it. From the way Chase kept shifting his weight, unable or unwilling to even place his hip on the edge of Sean's seat, to the utter silence from the other side of the cockpit, Foster knew Sean was dead. But Foster kept going. Clinging to the false hope that if he could stay awake — make it one more minute, one more mile — it wouldn't be in vain.

That he hadn't failed his brothers when they'd needed him the most.

That maybe one day, he'd be able to look at his own reflection and not see Sean's ghost staring back.

* * *

"I'm not sure what I was expecting, Foster, but damn. You look like shit. Though, the bandages do kinda go with the long hair."

Foster twisted toward the door, shaking his head at the man leaning against the frame. Hands shoved in his pockets, looking almost as haggard as Foster felt. Keaton Cole, Foster's cousin and the only family Foster had left, other than the men gathered in his room. His teammates.

His brothers.

Foster arched a brow, brushing his hair out of his eyes. A leftover from his time in Flight Concepts, when he was encouraged to look like anything but typical military. He gave Keaton a once-over, waving the length of him. "And yet, still a thousand times better than you, buddy."

"Oh, someone didn't get their pain meds, today." Keaton sauntered in, grinning at Chase, Kash and Zain. "You're obviously taking fashion cues from my cuz, Remington, because you look just as bad, with Sinclair and Everett only slightly better."

Chase flipped Keaton off as he leaned back in the chair. "At least we have a reason, Cole. What's your excuse?"

Keaton chuckled. "Civilian life. Who knew it was crazier than the Navy." He crossed his arms over his chest, waiting until Zain and Kash had wheeled their chairs over to Foster's bed. "So, rumor has it you four might be considering your options."

Zain grunted, absently rubbing his knee. Or more accurately, the new hardware hidden beneath the bandages and stitches. Foster wasn't sure if Zain even realized he was doing it, but the pain and frustration bled through his usual facade. Testament to how much their last mission had cost them.

Foster knew his buddy was in agony. He'd heard the muffled shouts and hushed curses as Zain dragged his ass up and down the hallways several times a day. The price of reclaiming even a hint of his former mobility. Though, Foster knew Zain would push until he was only a slightly broken version of his former self.

Zain shrugged. "It's come up."

Keaton nodded, walking over and resting his hip against Foster's bed. "I feel that. Been where you all are, myself."

Which was an understatement. Keaton had been through hell. Had suffered a similar loss on his last mission, when their covert op had gone off the rails and one his best friends had been killed. While Foster didn't know the specific details, he knew Keaton. And based on the hollow look in his eyes — the tremor in his voice that was only now starting to ease — he'd experienced something truly horrific. Not that it had been the first time.

Keaton's fiancée had been killed in an aerobatic accident a dozen years ago, shortly after he'd joined the SEALs. Foster had come close to losing the man back then, despite all Foster had done to try and help Keaton cope with the loss. But words and a shoulder were rarely enough compensation for the kind of scars that took more than time to heal.

Though, Keaton had more than paid Foster back when Foster's parents had been killed in a car accident a month ago. Foster and his team had been running those traitorous CIA assholes all over hell's backyard on one covert mission after another and he hadn't been able to extract himself long enough to head home. But Keaton had dropped everything and stepped up.

Foster would never forget that.

Foster shuffled back a bit, giving Keaton a thorough once-over. "I can't believe I'm saying this, but Florida looks good on you. You sound better."

Keaton sighed. "Getting there. Which reminds me... You should all come down for a visit. See the town. Get a feel for what we do. There's always room for guys like you."

Kash chuckled. "Are you suggesting we consider retiring to Florida?"

Keaton grinned. "Sunshine. Beaches."

"Gators. Mosquitos."

Zain swatted Kash across the chest. "And don't forget the pythons. I hear those fuckers grow really big."

Keaton rolled his eyes. "You've all been hanging around Foster for too long. The Everglades are fine."

"Sure, if you're looking to disappear." Chase pointed a finger at Keaton. "Permanently."

"Just, keep it in mind. Though, I suppose my dumbass cousin is trying to talk you all in to heading to Oregon, where there's nothing but gray clouds and rain."

"I'm not trying to talk them into anything." Foster shifted on the bed, not that it helped eliminate the pain throbbing through his shoulder. "But my parents did leave me that turn-of-the-century manor house they'd been renovating. Sounds like a good place to start."

Keaton laughed, nearly falling off the bed before he straightened. "You're going to fix up that old dusty inn? Are you all nuts?"

"Beats swimming with gators."

"You keep telling yourself that. Besides, Raven's Cliff is so small, you have to run to the next town to change your mind."

"And Calusa Cove is your idea of big time? I hate to break it to you, cuz, but it's just as small." Foster smiled. "And there're gators."

Keaton shook his head. "Still as stubborn as a damn mule. Though, I guess some things never change. Like us. Whether you're ready to face it or not, sooner or later you'll have to admit that we're all just hardwired differently. No way you'll be able to stay out of the fray for long."

Foster pursed his lips, Sean's gurgling rasp sounding in his head. Foster glanced over at the windows, hating the eerie apparition standing in the graying light. Blood still dripping from its neck and ribs as the ghostly image tapped its chest pocket.

It wasn't real. He understood that much. Just a by-product of the pain and anger and loss. Too bad that knowledge didn't make it disappear.

Keaton sighed at Foster's silence, looking over at the window then focusing on him, again. "Hey, didn't you mention something about an old JSOC commander of yours starting up a search and rescue organization there?"

Foster snorted. "Colonel Atticus Parker. Bastard's already called me twice. Wants to know when we're all signing up."

"And?"

"I told him I wasn't interested, but *no* isn't in the old man's vocabulary."

"Is this where we start a pool on how long it'll be before you've all been recruited?"

"About as long as it would for me to move down to the Everglades." Foster shifted again, but it only shot pain down through his ribs. "I don't suppose you'd do us a solid?"

Keaton laughed. "I already ordered a few pizzas. Just thought I'd stop in and visit while they were being made. I'll go grab them. Keep my seat warm."

His cousin headed for the door, pausing at the threshold. "Whatever you jerks decide, do yourselves a favor — stick together. Civilians really are crazy and knowing I still have my team watching my six is the only reason I've stayed sane." He made a finger gun at Foster. "That, and you, cuz."

"Just grab the pizzas before we all start puking."

"Your wish." Keaton headed out, leaving a strange void in the air. As if he'd taken most of the oxygen with him. Left nothing but uncertainty behind.

Foster cleared his throat, looking each of his buddies in the eyes. "I know we talked about calling it quits. Going to Oregon and seeing if a change in venue somehow fixes the broken parts the doctors can't splint. And there'll always be a place waiting there for you jackasses to hang your hat. But there's no pressure. Given some time and enough rehab, you all might—"

"Might what, Beck?" Kash shuffled in his seat. "Get the urge to jump back in the saddle? Put our lives in the hands of some traitorous agents, again? Because I don't know about Zain and Chase, but there's not a chance in hell I could go down that road, again."

Some of the color drained from Kash's face and Foster suspected he wasn't the only one reliving that night. Though, Kash had nearly lost his four-legged partner, Nyx, on the gauntlet run back to the chopper. Realizing she'd almost died in order to protect two traitors who'd then killed Sean and put Rhett in what might be a permanent coma had obviously affected Kash on a whole other level.

Kash sighed. "I'm not saying that staying on the sidelines is in the cards. But I'm ready to try something new. While I'm still alive enough to enjoy it."

Zain gave Kash's arm a pat. "What he said. We're all up for re-enlistment over the next two months. Seems almost poetic in the timing, if you ask me."

"Which is why we didn't." Chase dodged Zain's slap. "And you're not pressuring us, Foster. After everything that went down…" He swallowed, looking as if he might puke. "I think we could use a fresh start. Don't much care where that is, other than Florida. That's just wrong."

Foster nodded, a bit of the tension in his chest easing. "Then, it's settled. I'll contact the lawyer — get him to send over the papers he's been keeping for me. Just remember. I warned you all ahead of time that nothing exciting happens in Raven's Cliff. So, make peace with that. Things are about to get really boring."

If you want to read more of the exciting story
RAVEN'S WATCH click HERE

ABOUT THE AUTHOR

ELLE JAMES also writing as MYLA JACKSON is a *New York Times* and *USA Today* Bestselling author of books including cowboys, intrigues and paranormal adventures that keep her readers on the edges of their seats. When she's not at her computer, she's traveling, snow skiing, boating, or riding her ATV, dreaming up new stories. Learn more about Elle James at www.ellejames.com

Website | Facebook | Twitter | GoodReads | Newsletter | BookBub | Amazon

Or visit her alter ego Myla Jackson at
mylajackson.com
Website | Facebook | Twitter | Newsletter

Follow Me!
www.ellejames.com
ellejamesauthor@gmail.com

ALSO BY ELLE JAMES

Raven's Cliff Series

with Kris Norris

Raven's Watch (#1)

Raven's Claw (#2)

Raven's Nest (#3)

Raven's Curse (#4)

A Killer Series

Chilled (#1)

Scorched (#2)

Erased (#3)

Swarmed (#4)

Brotherhood Protectors International

Athens Affair (#1)

Belgian Betrayal (#2)

Croatia Collateral (#3)

Dublin Debacle (#4)

Edinburgh Escape (#5)

France Fallout (#6)

Brotherhood Protectors Hawaii

Kalea's Hero (#1)

Leilani's Hero (#2)

Kiana's Hero (#3)

Maliea's Hero (#4)

Emi's Hero (#5)

Sachie's Hero (#6)

Bayou Brotherhood Protectors

Remy (#1)

Gerard (#2)

Lucas (#3)

Beau (#4)

Rafael (#5)

Valentin (#6)

Landry (#7)

Simon (#8)

Maurice (#9)

Jacques (#10)

Brotherhood Protectors Yellowstone

Saving Kyla (#1)

Saving Chelsea (#2)

Saving Amanda (#3)

Saving Liliana (#4)

Saving Breely (#5)

Saving Savvie (#6)

Saving Jenna (#7)

Saving Peyton (#8)

Saving Londyn (#9)

Brotherhood Protectors Colorado

SEAL Salvation (#1)

Rocky Mountain Rescue (#2)

Ranger Redemption (#3)

Tactical Takeover (#4)

Colorado Conspiracy (#5)

Rocky Mountain Madness (#6)

Free Fall (#7)

Colorado Cold Case (#8)

Fool's Folly (#9)

Colorado Free Rein (#10)

Rocky Mountain Venom (#11)

High Country Hero (#12)

Brotherhood Protectors

Montana SEAL (#1)

Bride Protector SEAL (#2)

Montana D-Force (#3)

Cowboy D-Force (#4)

Montana Ranger (#5)

Montana Dog Soldier (#6)

Montana SEAL Daddy (#7)

Montana Ranger's Wedding Vow (#8)

Montana SEAL Undercover Daddy (#9)

Cape Cod SEAL Rescue (#10)

Montana SEAL Friendly Fire (#11)

Montana SEAL's Mail-Order Bride (#12)

SEAL Justice (#13)

Ranger Creed (#14)

Delta Force Rescue (#15)

Dog Days of Christmas (#16)

Montana Rescue (#17)

Montana Ranger Returns (#18)

Brotherhood Protectors Boxed Set 1

Brotherhood Protectors Boxed Set 2

Brotherhood Protectors Boxed Set 3

Brotherhood Protectors Boxed Set 4

Brotherhood Protectors Boxed Set 5

Brotherhood Protectors Boxed Set 6

Iron Horse Legacy

Soldier's Duty (#1)

Ranger's Baby (#2)

Marine's Promise (#3)

SEAL's Vow (#4)

Warrior's Resolve (#5)

Drake (#6)

Grimm (#7)

Murdock (#8)

Utah (#9)

Judge (#10)

Delta Force Strong

Ivy's Delta (Delta Force 3 Crossover)

Breaking Silence (#1)

Breaking Rules (#2)

Breaking Away (#3)

Breaking Free (#4)

Breaking Hearts (#5)

Breaking Ties (#6)

Breaking Point (#7)

Breaking Dawn (#8)

Breaking Promises (#9)

Hearts & Heroes Series

Wyatt's War (#1)

Mack's Witness (#2)

Ronin's Return (#3)

Sam's Surrender (#4)

Hellfire Series

Hellfire, Texas (#1)

Justice Burning (#2)

Smoldering Desire (#3)

Hellfire in High Heels (#4)

Playing With Fire (#5)

Up in Flames (#6)

Total Meltdown (#7)

Take No Prisoners Series

SEAL's Honor (#1)

SEAL'S Desire (#2)

SEAL's Embrace (#3)

SEAL's Obsession (#4)

SEAL's Proposal (#5)

SEAL's Seduction (#6)

SEAL'S Defiance (#7)

SEAL's Deception (#8)

SEAL's Deliverance (#9)

SEAL's Ultimate Challenge (#10)

Texas Billionaire Club

Tarzan & Janine (#1)

Something To Talk About (#2)

Who's Your Daddy (#3)

Love & War (#4)

Billionaire Online Dating Service

The Billionaire Husband Test (#1)

The Billionaire Cinderella Test (#2)

The Billionaire Bride Test (#3)

The Billionaire Daddy Test (#4)

The Billionaire Matchmaker Test (#5)

The Billionaire Glitch Date (#6)

The Billionaire Perfect Date (#7)

The Billionaire Replacement Date (#8)

The Billionaire Wedding Date (#9)

Cajun Magic Mystery Series

Voodoo on the Bayou (#1)

Voodoo for Two (#2)

Deja Voodoo (#3)

Damned if You Voodoo (#4)

Voodoo or Die (#5)

The Outriders

Homicide at Whiskey Gulch (#1)

Hideout at Whiskey Gulch (#2)

Held Hostage at Whiskey Gulch (#3)

Setup at Whiskey Gulch (#4)

Missing Witness at Whiskey Gulch (#5)

Cowboy Justice at Whiskey Gulch (#6)

Boys Behaving Badly Anthologies

Rogues (#1)

Blue Collar (#2)

Pirates (#3)

Stranded (#4)

First Responder (#5)

Cowboys (#6)

Silver Soldiers (#7)

Secret Identities (#8)

Warrior's Conquest

Enslaved by the Viking Short Story

Conquests

Smokin' Hot Firemen

Protecting the Colton Bride

Protecting the Colton Bride & Colton's Cowboy Code

Heir to Murder

Secret Service Rescue

High Octane Heroes

Haunted

Engaged with the Boss

Cowboy Brigade

An Unexpected Clue

Under Suspicion, With Child

Texas-Size Secrets

Made in the USA
Middletown, DE
09 August 2025